I0618999

Cappuccino Mugs & Fire Fighter Hugs

COFFEE LOFT SERIES

Katie O'Connor

–Cappuccino Mugs & Fire Fighter Hugs –
– Cherry Lake Fire Fighters Book 2 –

This book is a work of fiction. Names, characters, places, and incidents either are products of the author's imagination or are used fictitiously. Any resemblance to actual events, locales, or persons, living or dead, is entirely coincidental.

Published February 2024
(katieohwrites.com)

ISBN: 978-1-989816-76-9
Print: 978-1-989816-77-6

Cover art by Beck and Dot Cover Design
Editing by Terri St. Clair

Dedication

For Mom. I'm a terrible child and don't phone nearly often enough. Like you, I'm not much of a phone chatter. But know that you're in my thoughts every minute of every day. You are my strength and my heart. Your support keeps me writing. Love you muchly.

About this Book

Drinda McKenzie is struggling to stay afloat. She's just bought into in the famous Coffee Loft franchise. People in Cherry Lake are reluctant to take a risk on her shop and if they don't start coming by, she'll lose her life savings. Her favorite customer is a kindly matchmaker who thinks her grandson is the perfect man for Drinda. Too bad an outgoing guy like Ford would never be interested in a wall flower like her. Besides, he's her landlord and she's hiding a puppy in her no-pets-allowed suite.

Ford Langhammer is busy enough as it is, but when his grandmother keeps thrusting the lovely Drinda into his life, he's tempted to fall for her matchmaking schemes except he's a little wary of women after his last disastrous relationship. When his boss assigns him to help with Cherry Lake's Valentine's Ball, he's stuck in close proximity with Drinda. She's a wonderful woman, but after a brief flare of attraction, she's back away like she's up to something.

Will the magic of love join forces with an inveterate matchmaker and bring Ford and Drinda together, or will their differences over her wee puppy make them died in the wool enemies forever?

Chapter One

Drinda McKenzie smiled at the elderly customer with purple boots and an orange jacket. It was a great outfit for Halloween, but it was already January. Her gray hair was short and spiked up with golden tips. "Can I get you anything else, Mrs. Lunghamer?"

"I keep telling you to call me Franny, dear, and I would love a slice of that Black Forest cake." She patted her gently rounded belly. "Not that I need it, but the smell of fresh coffee and that chocolate are making me drool."

Drinda smiled at how the winter jacket's fitted design accentuated Franny's fit form. She packed up a slice of cake and set it beside the whole-wheat bread and gingersnaps her customer had already requested. Mrs. L. never left without her cake; she bought a slice on every one of her twice-weekly visits. She had since the day Drinda opened The Coffee Loft. "Mrs. Lunghamer, you look perfect."

"Thank you, dear."

Drinda tallied up the items, grateful for the continued support of her fledgling business. She smoothed her pink and blue coffee loft apron while Mrs. L. rooted around in her cavernous purse for her wallet.

"I love the cup wall," Mrs. L. said. "Remind me to get my girlfriend a mug for her birthday next month. She'd love the one on the left, second row from the top."

Drinda glanced at the twelve-by-twelve cube shelf on the far wall. Each cube was just large enough to hold a coffee mug or cup and saucer. She was proud of the collection she'd gathered for sale. Some had pithy quips, others were antiques or just plain pretty. They were a great source of income. "I have another of those in storage. I'll save it for you."

"Thank you, I appreciate it. Have you met my grandson yet?"

Holy steaming latte. She had only been in town for four months and open for three and people, well one person, were trying to set her up. "I'm not certain."

"Oh, you'd know if you met him. He's one hot stud." She waved her hand in front of her face. "Literally. He's a fireman. Shift supervisor. Tall, handsome, sexy blue eyes, black hair, pecs that won't quit. Strong arms, great guns." Her grin was irrepressible.

Drinda didn't know whether to laugh or be appalled at the comments. "I'll keep my eye open for him." Drinda had a pretty good guess which one the septuagenarian meant.

All of September Drinda had been swamped with renovating the old church she'd turned into a coffee shop. Then, she'd spent all of October and November sneaking peeks at the firemen as they worked on their rigs. With snowfall, she watched them shoveling and cavorting in the yard. The fire hall was less than a block away. From the window of the bakery, she could see the fire fighters' antics.

3

Over the past few months, she'd noticed at least a dozen different fire fighters. There were two women, half a dozen blonds, two redheads, one older gentleman, and several with dark hair. At least two of those were in relationships ... if she could judge their status based on the women she'd seen them around town with.

That left two men. One was short and stocky; the other was tall. Very tall, and from the looks of him, rock solid. She'd drooled over his biceps and shoulders more than once. Except for the tall, dark one, they'd all been in more than once for coffee and snacks. She was the closest food establishment to the station. The day the first snowfall came, she knew a moment of sadness that they would no longer be messing around outside where she could ogle them.

"Would you add two dozen assorted cookies to my order?"

She packed the treats and they completed the transaction. Mrs. Lunghamer scurried away leaving the cookies behind. "Mrs. Lunghamer, you forgot your cookies," Drinda called.

"Oh dear, call me Franny, and could you please deliver them to the fire station for me? A treat for our boys in uniform. I must run, I'm late for canasta. Take care, Drinda. And thanks." She waggled her fingers in a wave and was off like a shot. For someone who looked to be in her seventies, she moved well. She schemed even better.

Drinda sighed. She could hardly refuse to deliver the generous treat to the station. The cookies were bought and paid for, and she did offer delivery, but usually for a fee. Still, much as she was disinclined to meet Franny's grandson, Franny was her best customer. The only others who came even close were the firemen and local law enforcement officers.

She slipped into her jacket and boots before hanging a *back in five minutes* sign on the door. Locking up, she scurried down the street through the slush.

This week had been unseasonably warm and that heat, combined with the salt and sand the town maintenance department laced the streets with, meant everything was a sloppy mess. She glanced at her leather boots as she splashed across the intersection. They'd need a good cleaning tonight or she was risking the salt destroying their finish. She'd kept them perfect for three years and wasn't going to let one slushy day wreck them.

She hustled up the walkway and through the station door. The scent of antiseptic and cleaner lingered in the air. The walls were institutional cream with gray doors and frames. The dull palette was brightened by bold fire safety posters and nature prints.

She paused inside the entry.

"Hello?" she called out, doubting anyone could hear her amid the raucous laughter coming from the back room. She *could* leave the cookies on the table she saw through an open door.

"Coward," she whispered.

"Who's a coward?"

"Jeepers!" She clutched her chest with one hand, nearly dropping the cookies. She whirled toward the voice. There he was in person. Mr. Tall Dark and Handsome himself. Her breath caught. Holy cupcakes with buttercream frosting. He was a tall steamy latte for certain. Laughter glimmered in his deep blue eyes. A girl could get lost in eyes like that. *Sugar plums.* She was staring.

"Who's a coward?" he repeated a somewhat smug grin on his face.

She shook her head to clear her distraction. "Nobody. Don't you know not to sneak up on people? Especially being a fireman and all. You'll give someone a heart attack."

"I heard you come in and when you spoke, I assumed you were talking to me." He bowed slightly. "My apologies. A fire station is a safe place to have a heart attack." He winked and thrust out his hand. "We haven't met. You must be Drinda."

"How did you know?" She adjusted her grip on the cookie box and took his hand in greeting. He had a good strong grip. Firm, but not overbearing. Warmth flowed from his hand to her entire body. *Holy hot chocolate syrup.*

"I recognized The Coffee Loft logo on the box. I have to say, for a coffee shop, you make amazing cookies and cupcakes." He rubbed his tummy with the hand that wasn't still holding hers.

She pulled back gently but he didn't release her. Heat flowed up her arm and warmed her entire body until her face felt hot.

"We haven't been properly introduced. I'm Ford Lunghamer, shift supervisor ... for this shift and this station anyway. We aren't the only station."

"Hi," she said, wishing she didn't sound quite so breathless. "Your grandmother sent over these cookies." She yanked her hand back and thrust the box at him.

"Thanks!" The single word rang with gratitude and enthusiasm.

"You're welcome. I'll just be going now." She turned toward the door. "Nice to meet you."

"Ah, but we haven't met yet. I only know your first name. Hang on. I'll walk you back. I was just on my way to get coffee for everyone."

"Okay." What else could she say? She couldn't really refuse to walk with him just because her heart was thumping wildly.

"Hang on one sec while I grab my jacket." He strode into the office he must have come out of and was back in seconds, with one arm inside his jacket. "Tell me, Drinda of no last name, what brings you to Cherry Lake?"

"I own The Coffee Loft."

"That tells me what you do, not why you moved here?" His voice was light and inquisitive leaving her the option to ignore the question.

The bold question was a touch unsettling. Despite her better judgment, she found herself answering. "When I heard that Coffee Loft had franchises open, I investigated them. My friend told me about the chain. I love the idea of being linked with a recognizable chain while still having the autonomy to do my own thing. Each owner has the freedom to add what they want. I want to bake. I love coffee and sweets. The Coffee Loft is perfect."

"Do you ever answer a direct question?" He held the door open for her and they stepped out into the cool winter air.

She glanced at him. His wink showed he was teasing. Her pulse skyrocketed.

"I spent my summers here as a kid. Mom and Dad traveled a lot. They were archeologists. I didn't enjoy being practically alone on digs." She shuddered. "The dirt was awful. I spent winters in Colorado with Mom's parents, and summers here with Dad's mother. Cherry Lake feels like home. It always has."

He made an interested but noncommittal sound.

"Why are you here?" She reversed his question as they traipsed across the slushy street.

"I grew up here. Cherry Lake has a great fire department. One of the best in the country. I've been meaning to pop over to your shop," he said.

"I think everyone you work with has been here. Everyone except you." She unlocked the door and held it open for him.

"I try not to fraternize."

His statement struck a chord and her shoulders bunched. "What am I? The enemy?"

"Not exactly. But it is my job to give you your three-month inspection. The health inspector and I will make a spot inspection to see if you meet all the

10

codes." The station chief had conducted her pre-opening inspection, and she was expecting him for the follow-up.

"And that makes us enemies? Ridiculous." A skitter of nervous energy had her bounding behind the counter. *What if she failed the inspection?* She chided herself for the ridiculous thought. She read the rules. She'd taken the food handling classes. *For the love of pies, she was a Red Seal Baker.*

"Not enemies, but I like to keep a distance."

"You're telling me that in a town as small as Cherry Lake, you aren't personally acquainted with the businesses you inspect? I'm calling it shenanigans. What's your real reason for avoiding me?"

Chapter Two

Ford grimaced at her bold question. He should never have agreed to come get drinks for his shift. Now that he'd met her, it was clear that she was as lovely as the guys had said. Her open jacket revealed that she was fit. Her blonde and white-gold hair glistened in the shop's bright lights. Her beautiful blue eyes reflected her every emotion. Even watching from the side he'd been able to tell there was more to her moving to Cherry Lake than she'd mentioned. She had a very expressive face. He wanted to keep asking questions just to watch her face transform as she spoke.

He slid the paper with everyone's drink orders across the counter. There was no way he'd talk about his real reason for avoiding her. She glanced at the list.

"This will take a while. Can I get you anything while you wait?"

"I'll be fine, but thanks." He looked around the room. She'd done an amazing job of transforming the old church into a coffee shop. Most of the stained-glass windows remained, though the old, cracked ones flanking the front entry had been replaced with stained glass replicas of The Coffee Loft chain's logos. The blend of secular and religious images was unusual, but to his surprise they made an interesting combination that worked.

The glass display cases and the windows were clear and unmarked by fingerprints. The tables were neatly aligned. There was a clear, unobstructed path to the door and from where he stood, he could see clear through the kitchen to the rear exit. There was a small stage off to the right. He'd heard she hosted musical and author events. Last week his grandmother had chided him for not coming to her poetry reading here.

Nature photographs taken around Cherry Lake, and the lake itself hung in black frames against the creamy white walls. The pink and blue accents managed to look upscale rather than girly. It was a warm welcoming space.

She bustled around in her jeans and long-sleeved T-shirt. She looked cozy and welcoming. The themed apron added to that feeling. He stuffed his hands in his pockets and studied the display case. Three sliced cakes, cupcakes, muffins, and four types of cookies. This was as much a bakery as a coffee shop, and it smelled amazing. Chocolate, coffee, cinnamon, vanilla, and lemon combined into a mouthwatering temptation. His stomach growled.

"I heard that!" Drinda smiled.

The bright light in her eyes nearly floored him. *Holy smoking ashes.* "Maybe I should eat something."

"What can I get you? There's the menu." She waved to the wall above and behind her. She switched out the coffee filter and in seconds the rich scent of fresh coffee washed over him. She moved efficiently like she'd done this a million times, and she probably had. The grinder started, then the steamer. She filled and labeled mugs and placed them side by side on the counter. She paused to look at him. "Have you decided?"

"A breakfast sandwich with bacon, please." He honestly expected it to be premade.

"That'll take a second. Hang tight. How do you want the egg in that? Scrambled, or fried, and hard or soft?"

"Fried hard please."

She nodded and went into the kitchen. Dishes rattled and the scent of bacon filled the air. Two minutes later, she was back with the sandwich on a plate.

"I should have asked, but I went with toast rather than a bagel or English muffin." She slid the plate toward him. "Have a seat and I'll finish these drinks."

"Toast is perfect." He'd been thinking toast and it felt nice that she'd got it right without asking. He settled into a comfortable booth where he could watch her work.

The shop had a rough n-shape. You walked into the door with one leg of the n on either side. Over by the bandstand, there was a wall rack comprised of small cubicles. Each cubicle held a mug or cup and saucer. Each was different, except for a t-shape in the middle. One horizontal and one vertical row held pink and blue Coffee Loft mugs. The others seemed to be a random assortment. Maybe they were for sale. They'd

16

be great gifts. Grammie would probably love the one that resembled a dog.

Either he had been starving, or the sandwich was the best he'd ever had. It had something different in it, a spice he couldn't quite identify. It filled his belly with warmth and comfort. *Oh, good gravy. He was not feeling warm and fuzzy inside over a sandwich. Was he? If he was, this place must have a secretly seductive atmosphere. Not unlike Drinda herself.*

"Your order is ready," Drinda called, just as he finished eating.

"What do I owe you?" He carried his plate to the dish trolley near the counter.

She named a ridiculously low price.

"That can't be right," he objected.

"It's right. First responders get plain coffee free, and fancy drinks at half price. Food is ten percent off. Your sandwich is on the house. Sort of a welcome to Coffee Loft thing." Her cheeks pinkened.

"I can't accept that," he said. "It could be construed as a bribe."

Her brows pinched together, and her lips turned down. "Are you saying I'd bribe you for a passing mark on my inspection?" Her hands landed on her hips. She reminded him of his grade six teacher, all stern and serious.

"No offense intended." He resisted the urge to grin and held up his hands in mock surrender. "I don't take gifts from businesses. No gifts. No swag. No freebies. It's a rule that goes with the inspector job."

She wrinkled her nose. "And the coffee discount?"

"That I can take, as you give that to all the responders."

She slapped some keys on the register and the new total popped up. "Pardon me for trying to be nice," she growled and shoved the debit machine toward him. Her eyes flared with anger.

She slipped the eight drinks into trays and then set the trays into a low cardboard box. "Be careful, they'll slide around. I'll get the door." Her voice had a hard edge.

Ouch! He'd really annoyed her. He was tempted to apologize but didn't bother. It wasn't his fault. Rules were rules and he'd never risk his job for a free

18

sandwich, even a delicious one. He would, however, be back for another one.

"Thanks for the coffees. I know your drinks are always tasty and a great change from the sludge at the diner." The diner's coffee wasn't bad. It was more ... average. But compared to Drinda's it was dishwater. Grammie said something about custom roasted, ethically sourced beans.

"You're welcome."

He bit back a smile because she obviously was still testy. "See you around," he quipped.

She mumbled something about not letting the door hit his backside on the way out. He grinned all the way back to the station. Drinda had spunk, that was for sure. No wonder his grandmother kept singing her praises. Grammie L. wanted him hooked up and having babies for her to cuddle. She was a bigger nag than his mother and that was saying something.

He glanced over his shoulder at the converted turn-of-the-century church. It had a fresh coat of steel-gray paint that breathed fresh life into a once aged façade. The intriguing Drinda was nowhere in sight. Too bad.

She could be just the type of gal he was looking for. Except for the career thing. It was old-fashioned, but he wanted a stay-at-home wife. Someone who would devote themselves to his children and to him. The women he worked with would take a round out of him if they knew how he felt.

He wasn't against women working. He was all in favor of women, or anyone, doing whatever they desired. But he wanted what he wanted and was not going to compromise. He'd rather stay single.

But someone who could cook like Drinda? Tempting. Very tempting. Her quick wit and good looks didn't hurt either.

Chapter Three

Drinda stared at the line of high schoolers snaking across the shop towards the door. They were loud, so much laughter and catcalling, but not unruly. Last week a young jock in a football jacket had stopped by to pick up a cherry pie for his mother. The next day he'd been back with his friends. Every day the after-school crowd grew. If she didn't speed up service, the youthful crowd might chase away the seniors brought in by Franny. Drinda was even getting the odd office worker on their way to work. She couldn't risk losing her new customers.

This morning, Mayor Rundle had stopped by for Drinda's signature drink, a Bacon Maple Latte. Each of the franchises had its signature beverage, some hot, some cold. When she had spare time, Drinda was working on something cold and special for the summer months.

21

Drinda refocused on the drink she was making. She loved creating elegant coffees and chai teas, the smell of coffee and cocoa, the roar of the steamers, and the steady pulse of the grinder, all brought her heart to life. But why did kids have to make things so complicated? Who in the world wanted a no-fat, quad shot, salted caramel, white chocolate latte topped with full-fat whipped cream, toffee sprinkles, and marshmallow syrup? Gross! And how could they afford the drinks? As a teen, she'd never have managed.

"Hey, can I help?"

She looked toward the voice. A purple-haired teenage girl stood at the end of the counter. She had a pierced eyebrow and was dressed entirely in black. The only bright spot was the sparkling silver lightning bolt on her T-shirt. By Drinda's best guess, the girl had to be about sixteen.

Before Drinda could formulate an answer, the girl said, "I'm Maxi. I used to live in Seattle, where I worked for a coffee chain. I know what I'm doing. I'd really like to help you out." Her earnest expression of hope convinced Drinda to give the girl a shot. Heaven knows she needed help. She'd put an ad on the town hall bulletin board and social media pages, with no success.

"Let's see what you can do. Go wash up. You can hang your jacket in the back. The top drawer of the filing cabinet has aprons. Grab yourself one." She didn't fret over theft as she kept everything locked up tight. If Maxi could help push the kids through faster, it would be a blessing.

"Yass! You won't regret it." She fist-pumped the air and hurried into the back. Seconds later, she slid behind the counter tying up her pink Coffee Loft apron. "What's up?"

"Triple shot, non-fat, almond milk latte with vanilla syrup." Maxi's sure motions immediately revealed that she had indeed been a barista. They settled into a quick rhythm. Both making drinks while Drinda took orders and ran the register. Thank heavens she had two espresso machines and steamers.

Between bouts of the steamers' screaming, Drinda asked, "Have you taken food service training?"

"Not in Canada, but I can bring in my US certificate."

"If we go ahead with hiring you," she grinned to show it was a done deal, "you'll have to take Canadian training."

"No probs." She slid the drink she was working on onto the counter and called, "Order for Franny."

"Lovely to see you so busy," Franny called as she grabbed her cup. "I'll be back later for a snack. And look, there's my grandson now." She grinned and hurried past the remaining kids.

For the first time in over an hour, Drinda looked beyond the faces immediately before her. Ford Lunghamer, in full uniform, stood beside a man in a navy suit and tie. Both carried clipboards. Her inspectors. *Caramel crap.* They couldn't have arrived at a worse time.

She glanced around the prep area. It was untidy, but not disgusting. She knew the kitchen and back room were clean, but tables needed to be bussed and she might be over her occupancy capacity. *Sugar cubes.* She was done for. Why had they come on her busiest day, ever?

She met Ford's eye and smiled, though she wanted to frown and kick him back out the front door. He

24

showed absolutely none of the friendliness from his previous visit.

"Maxi," she hissed, "This is the health inspector and the fire inspector."

Maxi flew into action, wiping down surfaces and tamping down the garbage while Drinda made drinks with a racing heart and fake jolly demeanor.

She was congratulating herself on their quick work when the men stepped around the counter. She owed Maxi a debt of gratitude.

"Can I help you?" she asked with a welcoming smile.

She didn't greet Ford; she was still annoyed that he refused her free sandwich.

The other man introduced himself and handed over his business card. "Is now a good time for your inspection?" he asked as if she had the option of declining.

"Of course, it is. Just let me serve this drink." She lifted the frosty cup and to her horror, it slipped in her grasp and flew toward the men. It arced up, flipped end over end, and came back down.

Splat!

The inspector stepped out of the way, but Ford took the drink full in the chest. Whipped topping flew up and dripped off his chin as the icy coffee poured off his pecs, down over his stomach, and pooled under his boots.

"Oh no! Holy steaming mocha," she cried rushing toward Ford, rag in hand. Vainly, she tried to minimize the damage to his uniform.

"Leave it," he barked and grabbed the cloth out of her hand. "I'm fine. At least it wasn't hot."

"I'm sorry. It was an accident."

He gave her the stink-eye as if doubting the statement. So much for breezing through this inspection.

She turned to Maxi. "Can you take over please?" She explained the register before handing Ford more rags and scrubbing up the mess on the floor. It was ridiculously sticky, but proper cleanup could wait a few minutes. Drawing her dignity together, she turned to the men.

"Where would you like to begin?"

"We'll start in the back. If you could accompany us to answer any questions, it would help," the inspector said. Ford continued to glare. Ya, she was doomed.

"Sure thing. Right this way." She walked past them into the back, trying not to stumble when her knees trembled. She was more nervous than when she took her practical finals at cooking school.

Her kitchen was small. One double oven, three racks to hold finished items, or trays waiting to go in the oven. A sink, an industrial dishwasher, a cooler, and a freezer. The walls were white tile, and the counters were stainless steel. She leaned against the counter and let them wander around. She winced every time she caught a glimpse of Ford's sodden chest. With luck, he wouldn't be the type to penalize her for a small mistake. While Ford made dozens of notes on his clipboard, the inspector only made a few quick check marks on his.

Nothing missed the pair's attention, not the single stray wrapper on the counter, not the organized shelves in the storeroom and fridge, and not the carbon dioxide and smoke detectors.

"When was the battery in this last changed?" Ford jabbed a pen toward a CO_2 detector.

"It's hardwired with a battery backup. The battery was new when it was installed in October. I have my schedule marked to replace it in April. Every six months. Same for the smoke detectors." She bit back the urge to stick her tongue out at him.

The inspection was slow and tedious, but she managed to hold her patience at the micro inspection. Even the inspection she'd undergone before she opened wasn't this detailed. While the health inspector was satisfied, Ford continued to nitpick everything. Drinda kept one ear open for the front of the shop where Maxi was making drinks and ringing them through. Thankfully she didn't seem to be having any trouble. The girl was a lifesaver.

"You need to recharge those extinguishers. You can have it done at the station."

"They're good for another six months!" She stamped her foot. The man was utterly infuriating. The extinguishers had come with the space, likely left behind when the church closed last year. But they were valid.

"It's best to be proactive." The other inspector gave him a curious look.

"I've made a list of items that need attention," Ford said. "I'll be back in two weeks to check on your progress. You have thirty days to be fully compliant." He handed her a carbon copy of his report, nodded, and strode out.

"Who uses carbon copies these days?" she wondered. "I was expecting tablets and email."

The health inspector laughed. "My tablet died. That's why I'm using paper. I'll get a new company tablet when I get back to the city. I will, however, mail you your passing statement. Everything looks good to me. I'm impressed at your cleanliness while this busy. I assume your staff have all taken the appropriate food handling classes?"

"Maxi is here today on trial. She has a US certificate. If I hire her, she'll receive the proper training."

"I watched her work. It's clear she knows what she's doing. She looks like a good risk to me."

"How did it go?" Maxi asked after the inspector purchased a latte and left.

"I passed the health inspection with flying colors, but I've got stuff to "fix" for the fire department." She made air quotes around the word fix. "I think he's just annoyed that I dumped that iced coffee on him." She started giggling. "I didn't know whether to laugh or beg forgiveness."

"He looked hilarious with the whipped cream on his chest," Maxi laughed and waved a hand in front of her face. "And holy hotness. That's one heck of a chest he's got."

Though she agreed entirely, Drinda sobered. "We can't be objectifying our customers."

The door chimed and Franny strolled in on a wave of cold air. Her grin was entirely too smug. "I hear you dumped coffee on my grandson." She chortled and looked like a kid in a candy store.

"It was iced coffee, and it was an accident." It was going to take a while to live the mishap down.

"He'll survive." Franny grinned. "Speaking of my grandson, I've managed to get you both on the committee for the Valentine's Day Dance."

"Um. No, thank you." *A committee? No way on earth. Never.* She didn't like group work. She never had. She had abhorred it since working with Jess Yang in grade two. More than one person could never make a decision. Working one-on-one with customers was fabulous, but committee work was out of the question.

"I think you'll change your mind when you hear that being on the committee is the only way to get The Coffee Loft hired for the desserts. This could be the big break your little shop needs." Her gentle tone revealed her genuine desire to help Drinda grow her business.

"It's getting busier."

Franny snorted. "Kids will run out of money before long. No sense of budgeting at all. Why else would they be buying those froufrou drinks? Mark my words, you don't want to miss this opportunity. If you nail this one, you'll be hired for more. One thing this town loves is a special event." She nodded like she'd just imparted world-saving wisdom. "The special events cooking staff is great with entrees, but they lack imagination for desserts. A person gets tired of the same old all the time. They need you to mix it up."

"Oh, you should do this," Maxi exclaimed. "What an opportunity."

Quickly, Drinda made introductions.

"What do you think?" Maxi asked. "I think you should do it. I can help make desserts. My grandma was an amazing baker and we baked together all the time. I have her recipe book too."

Indecision froze her in place. Baking she could handle. Working on a committee, not so much.

"Don't let this opportunity pass you by," Franny advised. "Being around my grandson is just a bonus. Who knows, maybe you two will hit it off, get married, and start popping out babies for me to cuddle."

"When you put it like that, no thank you!" Drinda proclaimed.

"Fine. Forget my grandson." Franny sighed. "Do it for your business."

She mulled the idea around for a minute as she packed up some cake for Franny. It *was* an opportunity too good to pass up, despite her dislike of group work. Maybe it would be different with adults. These people were probably on the committee because they wanted to make the event the best it could be. That would help, wouldn't it?

"Fine. What do I have to do?"

"Well to start, don't act like you are on your way to your execution." Franny quipped, making Maxi laugh. "There's a meeting tomorrow night at the community center. Seven o'clock. Bring cookies."

Chapter Four

Ford left the firehall and trudged down the block toward the community center, keeping his eye open for icy patches. No sense taking an unneeded tumble. He hunched his shoulders against the brisk winter wind.

He'd successfully managed to resist his mother and grandmother's pestering to join the Valentine's Day committee. But when his boss had stepped in and suggested he join, he caved to the pressure. Grown men shouldn't have to be involved in this stuff. Valentine's Day was a chick thing. Men just went along to keep women happy. Even his father agreed. He'd only booked a Valentine's vacation to Europe to get his wife off his back. The hypocrisy annoyed Ford, even though he knew that a real man did things he might not otherwise do to please the woman he loved. Love was give and take.

Ford didn't have a wife or a girlfriend. Not that he didn't want them, he did. He wanted both, in the right order of course. Shiftwork kept him busy, and Cherry Lake wasn't exactly swimming in young single women.

He strode past the tall steepled church that housed The Coffee Loft thankful that he never had to go there again. Except for inspections, and those he could try and foist off on someone else. He shouldn't be so annoyed, but he was certain she'd dumped that drink on him deliberately. Drinda stirred up more than anger in him. There was an irresistible fascination as well, but she was a career woman, and that took her right off his radar.

Behind him, a bell chimed. He looked over his shoulder. Drinda. She was bundled into a knee-length navy jacket and headed his way. He pretended not to notice her and kept walking.

Her steps were brisk and definitely in his direction. They sped up and she called out, "Hey, Ford. Wait. We might as well walk together."

Blistered burns! He paused and rolled his eyes. "Evening, Drinda."

"Ford?" She grasped his arm and looked up at him.

She was shorter than he realized, probably six or seven inches shorter than his six-three. Why hadn't he noticed that before? Compared to him, she was small and cuddly, and too much temptation.

"I want to apologize again for dumping that drink on you. It wasn't intentional. Total freak accident."

"It isn't a problem. Accidents happen." The earnest entreaty in her eyes almost convinced him that she was seriously apologetic and not just begging forgiveness so she would receive a passing review. Not that he'd ever mark her harshly because of an accident. He wasn't that kind of guy. *He hadn't done that, had he?* He winced as a whisper of guilt pushed at his guts.

"We might as well walk together." She dropped her arm and gestured ahead. "We're going to the same place." She tightened her red plaid scarf, pulled her pompom-topped red knit cap lower on her head, and grinned.

'What? Where are you going?"

"To the planning meeting, of course. Your grandmother said you were on the committee. It's very generous of you to help."

"Thanks. You too." Too bad he was only doing this because he had to.

"Thanks. I'm nervous about all the people. I'm not good with crowds. I'm good one-on-one or in the shop. You know how that is, I'm in charge there. Plus, I'm good at what I do. That makes me strong. But take me out of my element, and I'll get an attack of the nerves and won't know what to say or how to act. I'm sure I'll do something stupid and nix my chance of getting a contract for the desserts. Of course, the contract isn't the only reason I'm doing this."

She sucked in a breath, and he thought she was finished speaking.

Nope.

"I'm doing this to get to know my neighbors. I spend so much time at the shop that my social life is non-existent. I mean I don't do anything but bake and make coffee. Don't misunderstand. I love what I do, but The Coffee Loft is my whole life." She sighed. "But it shouldn't be. I'm more than just coffee."

"You're coffee and chatter?" He grinned. "Nervous?" he asked, already knowing the answer.

"Yup. How could you tell?" Her light chuckle made him smile. She wasn't holding a grudge over his harsh evaluation, though maybe she should be. He'd been a heel.

"Just a guess." He smiled. "Don't fret about the people. Everyone in Cherry Lake is pretty easygoing. I admit, there are a few gossips and one or two grouches, but the chances of them being here are slim. Community events all tend to be run by the same crew. One or two change out depending on the event, but for the most part, it's the same group of good people. You have nothing to fear."

"Nothing to fear except making a fool of myself. What if we can't agree on things? Then what? Do you have any idea how many people have commented on that spilled coffee?"

Heard about it? He'd heard about nothing else all day. There was even a hand-drawn cartoon meme on the Cherry Lake social media page. He felt bad about that. Time to change the subject. "What's in the box?" He nodded toward the string-tied Coffee Loft box she carried in one mittened hand.

"Cookies for the committee. Your grandmother's idea."

"Grammie L. does love her sweets. It's a good thing she loves to walk and do yoga. Otherwise, she'd be dangerously overweight. I worry about her; she's not getting any younger."

"She gets around amazingly well. How old is she? She looks like she's in her early seventies."

"Eighty-three. I can't believe she still lives in her own house, and alone too." He shook his head. He worried about his elderly grandmother, despite her being much more fit and active than many her age.

"She looks amazing. I never would have thought she was that age. Do you do her yard work and shoveling? You seem the type."

What did that mean? Was it a compliment? It sounded like one.

"I can't deny helping. The department has a shoveling and lawn care group. We pitch in to do what others can't. Grammie L. is on the list. I even do her gardening. She loves flowers and fresh vegetables. She tells me what to do in the garden, and how to do it, and supervises and critiques while I follow her directions."

"Aw. That's so sweet. You're a good guy, Ford Lunghamer."

"Thanks, Drinda." He paused mid-step. "I just realized I don't know your last name."

"Interesting." She kept walking, leaving him behind.

"Aren't you going to tell me?"

"A girl needs her secrets."

"What? It's a name," he declared. She was being ridiculous.

"Haven't you read *Rumpelstiltskin*? There's power in a name," she teased and took off at a jog leaving him to catch up.

"Wait," was she really running away?

He raced after her, a surprised laugh spilling out of his mouth and filling him with glee. She got to the corner, paused briefly to check both ways, and hopped off the curb. "Slow down, the roads might be slippery under the fresh snow."

The words were no sooner out of his mouth than she lurched forward, arms windmilling wildly. The cookie box flew and landed with a thump, badly denting one corner. Drinda's feet slid in all directions like something out of a cartoon. They skidded forward in one final slick motion, and she started going down. Backward.

He stretched out as far as he could and barely managed to grab the shoulders of her navy pea jacket and kept her from landing on her backside in the snow. Unfortunately, his feet flew out behind him, and he went down.

Hard.

Face first.

His elbows smashed into the icy road; his stomach hit with a breath-robbing thump.

Drinda landed right on his head, driving his chin into the road. *Son of a pile of smoking rubble.* He groaned as his breath rushed out.

"Mphf," he grunted. Cold dampness seeped into his jeans, chilling him through in seconds. He shivered and struggled to get out from under her. She was heavier than she looked.

Drinda scrambled off him. "Oh my gosh! Are you okay? You totally should have let me fall!" She offered her hand as he rolled over.

Mistake! Now his backside was cold too. Shivers danced down his spine and back up the front of his entire body. Grabbing her hand, he struggled to his feet. His chest ached as he gasped for breath. "You're an accident looking for a place to happen," he ground the accusation out.

"How is it my fault?" She stomped her foot and glared.

"You ... ran off ... without thinking ... about the ice." He gasped. "I tried to save you." He bent over, put his hands on his knees, and sucked in a breath. Why did it take so long to breathe after you had the wind knocked out of you? He wasn't prone to emotional outbursts, but by all that was safe and good, he wanted to shake some sense into her.

"What's the big deal? I'd have landed on my backside. Maybe bruised my tailbone. Frankly, Ford, you need to loosen up. Your spine's so stiff you probably can't bend enough to tie your shoes."

She stomped further into the street, picked up her cookie box, brushed it off, and kept right on going. He hobbled behind, massaging his aching elbows. He wasn't wet, just danged cold. He might as well go to the meeting. There would be coffee and cookies ... at least there would be cookie crumbs. Since Drinda had baked the cookies, even the crumbs would be delicious.

He was not going to the meeting because she fascinated him with her good looks, her skills, her confession of shyness, or her ability to laugh and play. It wasn't because she was a good businesswoman either. He was doing this to shut his grandmother and boss up. Wasn't all the lawn mowing and snow shoveling enough community service?

Why was Drinda going? Her shop was getting busier by the day. That proved she knew what she was doing. If she was messing up orders, or the drinks were bad, nobody would come back. Except maybe his grandmother who was bent on getting Ford and Drinda together. His grandmother was something else. Exasperating at times, but always good-hearted.

He had the irreverent thought that maybe Drinda's last name was Christie, because like the old ads said, "Mr. Christie, you make good cookies." She made exceptional cookies. Naw. Drinda Christie didn't have the right ring to it. Maybe she was a Keebler Elf.

He shook his head at the ridiculous thoughts. Something about Drinda made him scatterbrained and curious.

Drinda was seated beside his grandmother, a steaming mug in front of her by the time he arrived. Okay, so he'd deliberately delayed his entry. If he showed up with Drinda, his grandmother would get all kinds of ideas.

"Ford, about time you got here. I didn't hear any sirens. Was there an emergency at work?" Grammie L. asked, in her *what are you trying to pull* tone.

"No. Just enjoying the evening weather. The stars are amazing tonight. You can see them even with the streetlights." He wasn't lying ... at least not about the stars.

"And you held us up for that? Everyone else made it on time. Punctuality is important, dear." She nodded as if putting an end to the discussion. A few choice words, in that tone, and she made him feel like a naughty schoolboy.

He slipped into the only available seat at the folding table serving as a meeting table. He wedged himself into the tight space between his grandmother and Drinda. Whoever set it up should have used two tables. It was so cramped his shoulders kept brushing Drinda's; that, and her strawberry-coffee scent was alluring and distracting.

"Let's call this meeting to order," Nathaniel Brooks, committee chair, declared with a smile. His brilliant white teeth shone against his dark skin. "Since we've all tasted Drinda's baking, it's safe to say she has the contract for dessert. What are you planning?" The committee chair turned to Drinda.

"Oh. I haven't put much thought into it yet. I'd like to go somewhere different with dessert. A lot of these events serve pie, or cake, like Black Forest cake. I was hoping to do something different. Tiramisu, a torte, maybe something chocolate-based, like truffles."

"What's wrong with traditional?" Ford interrupted.

Drinda glared at Ford. "What's wrong with mixing it up?" she asked, trying not to glare or grit her teeth. This was why she didn't like interacting in groups.

Disagreements always came up and she detested them because she had no idea how to react.

"What's wrong with traditional?" he repeated his earlier question with a mocking smirk.

Heat rose in her face. The man was infuriating. He annoyed her every time they interacted. "There's nothing wrong with traditional, but a change can be nice."

"True," his grandmother put in. "We're skipping the traditional roast beef dinner, and steak and lobster, this year. We're going with Beef Wellington, which we've never done before. It was a toss-up between that and fondue. Why not mix everything up? It might draw in a bigger crowd."

"We have plenty of time to plan dessert," Nathaniel said. "In fact, we'll leave that to Ford and Drinda to work out. We'll get you two to bring back a plan when we meet in two weeks. Now, let's move on and talk decorations."

Drinda fumed. Not only was Ford her inspector, but now she had to work alongside him for dessert planning.

When everyone pushed back their chairs to leave, she realized she'd been so busy fuming she hadn't heard a single word that was said. She had no idea what plans had been made and what decisions had been postponed.

"Franny, can you stay and catch me up? I got lost thinking about desserts," she said.

"Oh no, dear. Sorry. I'm in the middle of watching a documentary on television and I don't want to miss it. Egypt you know. Fascinating. I'm heading there this summer with a friend. Cairo, the great pyramids, the temple of the bulls. I'm sure Ford will help you out. You two have a lot to discuss."

Easy as that, she found herself walking toward home, Ford at her side. "I'm sure this is out of your way," she said.

"I told Grammie L. that I'd walk you home and discuss the meeting. I won't go back on my word. Besides, Cherry Lake is a small town. Like you, I walk most places."

She sighed. "Okay." How did he know she preferred walking over driving short distances? "This way," she pointed down the street.

Their steps tapped loudly on the frozen concrete and echoed into the silent starlit night. They ambled down Main Street, past The Coffee Loft, past the fire hall, and the hardware store. The night was too peaceful and beautiful to rush home. Sounds of sweet harmony came from the Catholic church. She paused for a moment to enjoy the melody.

"They sound amazing," she said as they strolled into the residential area. "They wowed me at the Christmas service last year when I was visiting."

"It's getting colder," she stuffed her hands deeper into her pockets. "I wish there was more cloud cover to trap the heat."

"Clouds mean snow. Last year, Old Man Sedgewick's roof collapsed under the snow load. It was a darn good thing he was at the pub when it happened."

"That's terrible. I mean I'm glad he was okay, but to lose your house ...."

"Everyone pitched in and rebuilt it. Insurance covered the materials. Still, excessive snow causes trouble."

"Are you always like that?" she asked. "Do you always see the worst? Like my not even close to expired fire extinguishers?" She wasn't an unbeatable optimist, but neither was she a pessimist.

"I just believe in safety." He bit the words out. His tone reminded her of a snapping dog.

"I suppose that makes sense, being a fire fighter and all." Two blocks of uncomfortable silence later she said, "Well, this is me." She waved toward a gray and white, two-story duplex.

"No kidding?" He laughed. "This is me too. We're neighbors." His tone implied that he knew they lived side by side.

Though she was rarely home, she had thought it odd that she'd never met her neighbor. "I've never seen you around. You rent here too?" She tried not to sound accusatory, but it felt weird knowing the man who held the future of her business in his hands lived next door.

"Sure. Go with that." He shrugged as they walked up the central sideway to the point where it branched toward the separate front doors.

"What does that mean?" She puzzled over his words. "You *own* this building? Tell me you only own one side." She didn't want to add landlord to the ways he was buried in her life.

He smirked. "I own this entire building, and that one, and that one." He pointed to two adjacent buildings. "Ten rental units in all. I have a rental company and my staff takes care of the details. Plus, a small strip mall out by the highway."

Just her luck! Things just got better and better. It was bad enough that she couldn't afford to buy a home, the franchise, and the church, but to have the man who held her business in his hand also in charge of her home was beyond all thinking. *He practically controlled her entire life!*

"A fire fighter, an inspector, and a slum lord?" she quipped. Hopefully, he'd know the last bit was a joke.

"Not a slum lord, a property owner. Yes, I'm all those things, and I also teach self-defense." His shrug was eloquent and self-deprecating. "Can I make you a cup of tea?"

She reared back at the surprise offer.

"I know it's nearly eight-thirty and you get up early. But I need to unwind. I feel like I was sucker punched at the meeting, and I'm still cold from lying on the ground. I thought maybe tea would be nice. Or a cup of decaf. Though I doubt I have your coffee skills."

She considered the offer and took it as the olive branch it appeared to be. "I could drink a decaf. Do you have cream?"

"I have milk?" He made the reply a question.

"Let me grab cream and I'll pop over." *After she had a moment to steady her nerves.* Ford stirred up something inside her she didn't want to acknowledge. Something that wasn't just anger or frustration. Something warm and welcoming. Occasionally, he seemed like a nice guy. She needed time to deal with the turmoil before seeing him again.

"I'll put a pot on. Let yourself in when you get back." In unison, they turned toward their own adjacent doors, unlocked, and went inside.

She eased the door shut and leaned back against it. Her breath whooshed out in a huff. She started giggling. Her life was completely and totally out of control. Moving to Cherry Lake had stirred things up. She came home to be close to her grandmother who lived in a senior's condo. They'd only managed one visit before her grandmother, friend, and confidant went on a whirlwind trip. She had nobody to vent to and her nemesis was a very attractive man who lived next door. Absurd!

Opening a new business was time-consuming and Drinda was almost run off her feet at work. While that was a blessing, it was exhausting. She needed more staff but didn't want to jump the gun. Especially not with her unpassed fire inspection hanging over her head. She still wasn't certain the bad mark wasn't due to Ford being annoyed at her.

And she'd gone and knocked him down tonight. And argued about dessert. What next? All that just made his offer of a nightcap ... unnerving. And confusing.

"Tough cookies, Drinda," she chided herself, "You said you'd come for coffee, you're committed. Yeah, I should be committed for accepting." She sighed and slipped out of her boots. She grabbed cream and a couple of butter tarts and headed to Ford's. "Might as well get this over with."

Chapter Five

Ford wiped down the counters and paced back and forth in the kitchen as he waited for the coffee to brew. Decaf. When was the last time he'd had decaffeinated coffee? Never. Shiftwork took a toll on you unless you learned to sleep at the drop of a hat ... even when you were riddled with caffeine. He only kept decaf on hand for his mother, it was all she'd drink. Grammie L., on the other hand, wouldn't be caught dead drinking decaf.

"Why did you invite her over?" he muttered as he leaned on the counter and watched the heavenly-scented dark brew drip into the carafe.

"I wondered that myself," Drinda said, coming into the kitchen.

"Whoa! I didn't hear you come in." He jerked upright.

"You said let yourself in ...." she trailed off. "Why *did* you invite me? It's not like we get along."

He stopped pacing to face her and rooted around in his mind for an answer that made sense. "I don't know. We're neighbors. We live in the same town. We're on a committee together." He shrugged. "It seemed like a good idea."

His honesty was refreshing. "Nice to meet you, neighbor. I brought tarts." She set them and the cream on the table and looked around. "Nice place. I love the table." She stroked the polished oak. "Is this an antique?"

Ah! Something they could talk about. He grasped at the topic of conversation like a drowning man reaching for a life preserver. "It is. It was my other grandmother's, not Grammie L. I refinished it. What do you think?"

"Exquisite." She squatted and inspected the pedestal base. "It's flawless. Do you do a lot of refinishing?"

"I've done a few pieces. It's a hobby." As she sat, he poured coffee for them both and brought the heavy, hand-crafted, ceramic mugs to the table.

"Thank you." She slid the cup closer. She looked around. The kitchen was tidy, and void of personality.

The heavy leather recliners and dark wood occasional tables she'd passed on her way in looked in good shape and uncluttered. "It doesn't look like a bachelor pad in here at all." She grinned at him as she poured cream into her mug.

"Thanks?" She had a knack for making him uncomfortable. "What were you expecting? Dirty socks everywhere? Pizza boxes?"

"Something like that," she quipped. "You know the stereotype. Though recliners instead of couches don't surprise me. Total mancave vibe."

"I'll have you know; I keep my place clean." He grinned though the mancave comment stung a bit. He didn't have trinkets everywhere so what? His home was comfortable. "I have a lady come in twice a week. I detest cleaning up almost as much as I hate a mess."

"Cheater." Her laugh rang out unfettered. Short, loud, and happy. No delicate laugh here. Just a quick bark of emotion. Delightful.

"I love your laugh," he admitted.

"Um, thanks?" She seemed surprised by the comment.

"That's a compliment." He paused to consider his next words before confessing, "I dated a woman, another fire fighter trainee. Years ago, obviously. She never laughed. The best I ever got was a smile."

"Never?"

"Never. She grew up being told that loud laughter was rude and uncouth. She learned to curtail the sound. Nothing makes me smile more than other people's laughter."

"Maybe I should have laughed when I spilled that coffee on you," she deadpanned. "Maybe you wouldn't have been so mad."

Her wink shot straight to his libido. "Unfortunately, it doesn't work like that. I'm sorry I got annoyed." He straightened the tea towel hanging on the stove. He probably should change it out, it was getting grubby.

"Apology accepted." She sipped her coffee. "You make a decent cup of decaf," she admitted.

"I try. Glad you like it." He sat across from her and added milk and sugar to his mug. He stirred it and set the spoon on a napkin from the pile in the center of the table. "I was thinking Black Forest cake," he fired his opening shot in what he knew would become a battle.

"Crème Brûlée," she countered.

"Angel food cake with fresh berries and whipped cream." He leaned back and crossed his arms over his chest. It wasn't cake, but it was one of his favs.

"We live in Canada. The dinner is in February. Where are we getting berries that haven't shipped from California?"

"Good point." He spun his mug around in a slow circle until the handle made a full rotation. "Ice cream bar where you choose your flavor and toppings?"

"I do love those, but I'm hoping to showcase my dessert skills. The committee is hiring me to bake, not to put out sprinkles. We need to come up with something better."

"I don't see why cake or squares don't work then, they'll showcase your work."

Her brows knit together, and she sighed. Her fingers tapped on the side of her mug. "I need more time to think on this."

"Okay, let's change the subject," he agreed quickly. Maybe if he didn't push too hard, he could win the argument. He wasn't certain why he was dead set on a traditional dessert, but somehow it felt important. "Cats or dogs?"

"Rabbits." She laughed at his frown.

"That didn't answer the question."

"Sure, it does. I'd prefer a rabbit if I were having a pet. Or maybe a de-scented skunk. I've heard they can be potty trained."

"In that case, I'll let you have the rabbit."

"Generous of you." She grinned mockingly. "What's your choice?"

"Cat. They are way more intelligent than dogs. Probably something from the shelter, or a friend who had kittens. You know what I mean, one of those mixed breed cats."

"I like that. I never understood spending a fortune on a purebred if you weren't going to put the animal in shows. But, to each his own, and all that. And just FYI, dogs are more intelligent than cats and they aren't nearly as arrogant. Are you planning on getting a cat?" she asked.

"Probably not. I don't allow animals in my buildings, and it would be unfair if I had one and didn't let my tenants have any." He shrugged. He could easily change the rules, or simply make himself an exception, but at this point, he wasn't super hyped to have a cat.

She rubbed her hands together. "Next question. Chicken or beef?"

"Beef. There are many more choices in beef than in chicken. Roasts, burgers, steaks, ribs. The list is endless."

"I'll take chicken any day. Fried, baked, roasted, grilled. Battered and deep fried. And you can't forget chicken wings with ranch dip."

They went back and forth asking questions, slowly getting to know each other. They shared a passion for detective shows, particularly old ones like *Barney Miller* and *Kojak*. They were both avid readers. Ford preferred action novels while Drinda preferred cozy mysteries. They fell into an easy, friendly, camaraderie though he couldn't forget how attractive she was. Her smile, her shining blue eyes, and easy laughter.

Drinda thought about his questions before she responded as if the answers mattered. She was easy to talk to as well as being easy on the eyes. Being with her reminded him that he wasn't getting any younger and needed to light a fire under his ambition and search for a woman to spend the rest of his life with. No more waiting for her to show up, it was time to start seriously looking.

"Holy smokes," he declared when he realized it was almost midnight. "It's late. I'm on the early shift tomorrow, and so are you. We better call it a night."

She yawned. "You're right. Five a.m. comes too soon."

"Why so early? You don't open until seven." He picked up their mugs, rinsed them, and loaded them in the dishwasher. Her smile of approval was sweet.

"I open at seven for the early birds on their way to work. I like to have fresh muffins by then. I need to roast some beans and it'll take me a couple of cups of coffee to get my brain in gear. I'm a slow starter."

"And yet you picked a morning career."

"Yeah," she said wryly. "Maybe not the best choice. Once I'm fully up and running, I'll be able to hire more staff and come and go as I please. I love coffee, baking, and being my own boss. And I love people in small numbers."

"You did well at the meeting. You didn't freak out or anything."

"No, but I zoned out a bit. I totally forgot. You were supposed to fill me in on what I missed," she frowned, sounding surprised.

As much as he was curious, he didn't ask what she was thinking of to cause a frown. They'd gone from uneasy and combative to something resembling friends and he didn't want to jeopardize that. "I'll fill you in on the meeting later. You didn't miss much at all."

He walked her to the door and helped her into her coat. She didn't button up. He wanted to tell her she should but held his tongue. While he didn't want her to catch a cold, it was only steps to her door. When his coworker lived next door they never even bothered with jackets when going back and forth. She'd be fine even without a jacket. His concern was what he'd feel for a sister, only stronger.

"Good night. Thanks for the coffee and conversation." She stepped out onto the front porch. He followed.

"What are you doing?" she gave him a puzzled look.

"Making sure you get inside okay." He shrugged.

"I literally live ten steps away."

"It's winter. It's cold and slippery. I'd never let a woman find her way home."

"Wow. Chauvinist much?"

"Not at all. It's courteous. I do it for Mom and Grammie L. Why wouldn't I do the same for you? Now, go inside before I freeze my toes off. Good night, Drinda. It was nice getting to know you." Better than nice. She was sweet and funny.

"Good night, Ford." She hurried down his steps, across the short distance to hers, jogged up, and unlocked the door. He didn't go inside until she shut the door behind her.

A yawn hit him as he flipped his deadbolt. Wow. He was exhausted, yet he hadn't noticed while they were talking. Interesting. He shut off the lights and trudged wearily up the stairs, brushed his teeth, and crawled into his bed.

The night was silent except for the soft sound of someone singing. He raised on one elbow. Drinda was belting out a tune next door. He'd never noticed she made any noise. She was a quiet neighbor. He leaned back down, a bit closer to the thick firewall separating their homes.

He drifted off some time after she sang *Bohemian Rhapsody*.

Chapter Six

Annabelle, the owner of Belle's Beauties, a lingerie shop down the street, burst through the door with a crooked smile and stamped the snow off her sturdy winter boots.

"Annabelle!" Drinda exclaimed. "I wasn't expecting to see you. What are you doing here?" She rushed from behind the counter to embrace her friend. They'd grown close in the time since Drinda opened, but it was unusual for her to stop by in the middle of the morning.

"I really need coffee. Can I get my usual?" she asked in her sweet and sunny Australian accent. She unwrapped her purple scarf and unzipped her puffy fuchsia jacket. A shake of her auburn head sent a shower of fluffy snow drifting to the floor.

"One lofty caramel macchiato coming right up. Extra whipped cream today?" Her friend had a sweet tooth.

"You better believe it. I can't stay long. I locked up the shop to come over. I've got ten minutes, max. But desperation was setting in."

"What's made you so desperate? Bad morning?"

"My coffee maker died. That was after I got stuck on my way to work. I can't believe how much snow has accumulated in the past week." She grimaced. "I called the tow truck, but it's out by the lake. Somebody put their SUV into the ditch. I can't believe Cherry Lake only has one working tow truck."

"Yeah, although I hear Andre has ordered two more. How did you get unstuck?"

"I got lucky. Ford Lunghamer drove by." She laughed. "I don't know why I use his last name all the time. It's not like there is more than one human Ford in town. Anyway, he called a couple of guys, and they pushed me out of the drift. He's so swoony." She clutched her chest and sighed.

"You totally should date him," Drinda offered as she poured espresso into a takeout cup. She meant the words until she uttered them. Once they were out, an uneasy sensation settled in her heart. *Was this jealousy? Couldn't be.*

"Date Ford? Not me. I mean, he's hot and all but we tried dating last year before you moved here. We just didn't click. Besides, I want a career now, and a husband and kids eventually. He wants a stay-at-home wife. That's not going to be me ever! Ford will make a great father and husband. Just not for me."

Drinda thought about Ford as she drizzled caramel overtop the foamy beverage. He was handsome, there was no denying that, and he was easy to talk to. But who wanted to be a stay-at-home mom these days? She didn't have a problem with the idea if that's what you wanted. It just wasn't a future she envisioned for herself. Bringing her kids to work with her at the shop was more her style. They would grow up in the business, loving baking. Just like she did.

"Drinda. Drinda! I think that's enough syrup!"

"What?" She tipped the squeeze bottle up and glanced at her friend.

"You've given me at least triple syrup. I'll weigh six tons if I drink all that."

"Sorry. I was distracted. My mind just isn't where it should be today. I probably need coffee. Like a triple espresso." As if anyone would believe a coffee shop owner was short on caffeine.

Annabelle's eyes lit up. "You were thinking about a certain hunky fireman!"

Drinda mock sniffed. "That's fire fighter, to be perfectly PC."

"Pfft. Fireman, fire fighter? What's the difference? Semantics. Language isn't my big thing. I'm into slinky fabric and sexy lace." She waggled her eyebrows up and down and struck a pinup pose.

"Here's your drink. This one's on me since I ruined it with too much syrup." Besides that, she wanted to change the tide of the conversation.

"You can't keep giving away drinks, but I'll accept it. And there is no such thing as too much syrup. I might need a sandwich for later ... to counteract the sugar crash that'll hit me an hour from now. I think I'll run to the deli and get one. Need anything?"

"That'd be great. I'll take a pastrami on rye with mustard and mayo. No veggies."

Annabelle saluted with her cup and left. Drinda threw herself into baking a batch of chocolate chip cookies. She had a great slice-and-bake version. The beauty of slice and bake was that it was easy to bake more later with almost no effort. She kept a good stack of customers' favorites frozen and ready to go.

She sang along with an old Keith Urban song as she worked. It seemed like only seconds before she heard Annabelle's voice.

"Hey, get away," Annabelle demanded, trying to wedge herself through the half opened front door. "Shoo."

"What's going on?" Drinda hurried from behind the counter.

"This crazy dog keeps trying to get inside. I barely got past him earlier."

"Oh no, don't let him in. He can't be in here." She helped her friend inside and stared at the mixed breed black and white puppy. "He's adorable, but he looks half-frozen. Look at the size of his feet. He's going to be big when he grows up. If he gets in here, I'll lose my license. Maybe I should call the town office. Is there an animal control officer here?"

"No. The police and fire department handle it, unless it's a wild animal, then they call Fish and

71

Wildlife." Annabelle handed her the package with her sandwich.

"What do I owe you for the sandwich?" she asked, not really paying attention, she was too focused on the black and white dog. He was large, but all puppy. Part husky, maybe some retriever or lab. She hated the idea of him shivering outside. Today wasn't too cold for a furry animal, barely freezing. But if the temperature dropped further, or he had to be outside too long, the poor dog would be in real trouble. He better go home soon.

"The sandwich is on me. Fair trade for the coffee. How are you going to keep him outside?"

"What?" She turned to Annabelle. "I guess I'll just make sure he doesn't sneak in and chase him out if he does." The idea of the poor pup shivering outside, maybe hungry, broke her heart. Maybe she should put up a poster somewhere to help find his owner.

After her friend left, she called the radio station and asked the DJ to mention the pup, and then she put a notice on the Cherry Lake social media buy and sell page that he was hanging around outside her shop. Maybe his owners would see it and stop by to pick him up. She ignored the cartoon of her spilling the coffee on Ford.

The rest of the morning was spent shooing the pup back outside when he snuck in. He had to be attracted to the smell of food, or the heat. He was a slippery devil and kept squeezing in between people's legs, tracking in snow. Desperate to keep him out, she slipped on her boots and grabbed some bacon.

"Hey, little pup," she crooned as he munched on the first slice she tossed him. She fondled his neck. No collar or tags. Dang, she was hoping to find his owner. With a second slice of bacon between her fingers, she lured him around the building to the back door. She tossed the slice into an empty cardboard box and hurried inside. Maybe he'd stay there, out of the falling snow, and away from the front door. The box wasn't much, but it would keep him out of the wind.

She stamped off her boots and slipped back into her snowflake print crocs. Unfashionable, but very comfortable. They were fur lined and cozy without being too hot.

"Hello?"

What was Ford doing here? Wasn't he working?

Which reminded her, she still had a couple of things to check before he returned for her follow-up inspection. *He wasn't here for that, was he?*

She hurried to the front.

Oh no! He was in uniform. This must be official.

"Good morning. How are you on this fine snowy day?" she blurted. "What can I get you?" She smiled her best, albeit nervous smile, silently praying he wasn't here for professional reasons.

"I've got a list." He waved a slip of paper.

She relaxed instantly and her shoulders slumped in relief. Coffee she could handle. "You do know that I have an app, right? You can order and it'll be ready when you get here."

"Actually, I didn't know that. Besides, if I used an app, I wouldn't get to talk to you while you made our drinks." His grin was all charm.

Something warmed inside her. Her heart leapt. Oh no! She was not interested in Ford that way. Nope. Not at all. And why was he flirting? He was flirting, wasn't he?

"Well, pass me your list and I'll get started." She barely kept her voice from trembling with nerves. His effect on her made no sense. He wasn't the first good-looking man she'd ever met or even the hottest. She sighed. There was still something about him that set her body fluttering. She'd been engaged for a brief time and even her fiancé hadn't had this type of effect on her.

"You've got snow in your hair," Ford commented. "Were you outside?"

"I just took some garbage out," she lied with a nearly straight face. She turned toward the coffee maker to hide the heat in her cheeks. She started a fresh pot of drip coffee. She'd learned quickly that many of the fire fighters and some older residents of Cherry Lake preferred plain old drip coffee. Accommodating them was easy and it kept them coming back.

She purchased excellent beans for roasting and they made rich, deeply flavored coffee no matter how she brewed it. Speaking of which, it was nearly time to roast a fresh batch. She'd meant to do that this morning, but it had slipped her mind.

"The snow is a pain," Ford said. "I've been pushing people out of drifts all morning. I was late for work because there were four people stuck between home and here." He shrugged. "I had no idea so many people were out that early."

"That's why I walked. I decided it was easier and less risky."

A dog barked.

Ford strode past the tables to peer out through the stained-glass window. "Hey, there's a dog out front. I don't see an owner. Somebody better round him up. It's chilly out there." He claimed not to be a dog lover, but his concern was clear.

Her stomach dropped and rebounded harshly. "I saw him earlier. I'm sure he's fine. Probably just ran out of someone's yard. I let the radio station know he's here." She didn't want Oscar to freeze, but she didn't want him taken away to a shelter either. She had no idea what local shelter policies were.

"I'll leave him for now in case his owners are looking for him. Let me know if he keeps hanging around, okay? We can't have Cherry Lake overrun with strays."

"I'll do that." The lie tripped off her tongue entirely too easily and she winced at her duplicity. She boxed up cookies, muffins, and one slice of pie as she waited for the coffee to brew. She was always amazed at the quantity of baked goods she sold. Before opening, she had expected hot drinks to be her main commodity, after all, she was a coffee shop.

Unable to resist, she inhaled deeply. The dark earthy scent tickled her nose and lifted her spirits. Overlaid with the aroma of fresh chocolate chip cookies it smelled like heaven.

Only two of the drinks in Ford's order were plain lattes. There was one cappuccino, and the other four were plain drip. Prepping them took only seconds per cup.

"What size is this Bacon Maple Latte?" She loved that someone was ordering her signature drink.

"The biggest?" He smiled as he came back from the window. "Thought I'd try it. You can't go wrong with bacon, am I right?"

"One Lofty Bacon Maple Latte coming up."

"Lofty? I thought coffee shops use names like venti and grande?"

"Not this one. I'm small, medium, large, and lofty ... in honor of The Coffee Loft franchise." She used her best haughty tone, and he laughed as she intended. His laugh was deep and bold. She couldn't help but smile. She loved a man with a sense of humor.

She placed the final cup in the cardboard tray. "You guys are recycling these, aren't you?"

"We are."

"Let me grab a box." She kept the flats from soda cans handy for holding large orders. She packed everything up for him. Drink trays on the outside, bags of baking between them. "If you bring the trays back, clean, we can reuse them for your next order." Her suggestion was met with a nod of agreement.

He nodded, paid his bill, and picked up the heavy makeshift tray. "Can you get the door?"

"Absolutely." To prevent accidents, she had the original solid wood doors modified to have glass panels. She peeked out before opening it. No sign of Oscar. Yeah, she'd named him the second she set eyes on him, or her, she hadn't taken the time to look at his privates.

"Have a good day, Ford. Thanks for coming."

"You too, Drinda. I'll see you at the planning meeting next week if I don't see you sooner."

"You bet." She opened the door and like a flash of lightning, Oscar shot inside. "Dang it."

"You better get that thing out of here. No animals allowed. It's a provincial regulation." He paused halfway out the door. "If he's a problem, call the town office and he'll be dealt with."

She hated the finality of his statement. "I'll do that," she lied without feeling the least bit guilty. The poor cold pup didn't deserve that type of treatment. Hopefully, his owners would find him soon.

"He should be inside someplace warm." Ford's soft-hearted comment as he walked away redeemed him.

"Here, pup. Come here," she called as she followed his snowy tracks to a table in the corner. He huddled under the padded bench seat made from a converted pew. "Come on out, Oscar." He backed further away.

"Silly mutt." She stood up as the front door chimed.

"What are you doing on the floor," Franny asked as she wiped her boots.

"Oh, nothing. Just looking for my earring."

"Let me help you look."

"Oh. No need. I just found it." She stood and pretended to reinsert the tiny dangling coffee cup earring.

"I'm glad you didn't lose it."

She hurried behind the counter and washed her hands. "What can I get you? And how are you this morning? Did you see Ford? He just left. He was in with a big order for the station."

Franny raised one eyebrow as if asking why she was babbling. "I'll have a chai tea latte and a butter pecan tart, please, and thank you." Franny had impeccable manners.

Drinda heated the milk for the drink and when she turned around, Franny had vanished. Where in the world?

"Did you know there's a dog in here?" Franny asked. She knelt by the bench and cooed at Oscar.

80

"Don't tell anyone. He snuck in when Ford left. I was trying to catch him when you came in. Do you recognize him?"

"Can't say that I do, not with him all huddled up like that. Do you have some meat or cheese? Maybe we can lure him out and see if he has tags."

"No tags," Drinda said with a sigh. "I checked earlier." She pulled some ham from the kitchen cooler and joined Franny on the floor. "I can't have him in here. I'll fail an inspection and lose my business."

"Shall we take him to the town office? Turn him in and hope someone claims him?"

"No!"

Franny stared at her.

"What if they take him to a shelter that isn't no-kill?" she whispered. "He's just a puppy." She waved the ham at the end of the bench. Oscar whimpered and inched closer.

"Oh, good. He's coming out." Franny edged back.

"Get ready to grab him so we can put him outside." She expected the immaculately dressed older woman to balk at the idea, but she looked eager to help. "Here, boy. Come on, Oscar. We won't hurt you."

"You know his name?" Franny gave her a puzzled look.

"I sort of named him when I first saw him." Heat filled her face.

"You're just a big softie. You should take him home with you."

"I can't. My landlord, your grandson, has a no pet rule." Oh, how she wished it were that easy. She'd love to have a pet. Of course, it wouldn't be fair to Oscar to leave him kenneled up all day.

An idea started forming in the back of her mind.

The pup wiggled close enough that she was able to grab him and cuddle him to her chest. "Good boy," she crooned as he nibbled the bacon. He snuggled against her and even though it nearly broke her heart, she set him outside the back door. "You stay out now. Go home. Go on. Go home, Oscar." She waved him away, but he just sat there, his eyes looking up at her, beseechingly.

There was no way in the world she was going to let Oscar end up in a shelter. She just had to figure out what to do with him. Maybe she could sneak him into her house without Ford noticing.

Katie O'Connor

Chapter Seven

Ford snuggled his winter cap lower on his head and tightened his scarf as he stood in the chilly air outside Drinda's door. "How did I get talked into this?" he muttered before he knocked.

Grammie L. That's how. Grammie had a way of adopting people and pulling them into the family. His grandmother always got what she wanted and today, she wanted a family dinner, with Drinda there.

Even more confusing was why Drinda agreed. He shook his head and knocked. The door opened immediately. "Are you ready?" he asked.

"Two seconds. I was just putting on my jacket." She shivered. "Come inside, it's freezing. Let me grab a scarf and warmer mitts." She dug through a small wicker basket under a cherry table near the door.

He stepped in and shut the door behind him. Her home mirrored his, but the effect was entirely different. Her fabric sofas looked soft, warm, and inviting in comparison to his pair of leather recliners. She had decorative pillows on the plush loveseats. Her coffee table held a bushy fern and several fat candles. A dim light glowed in the kitchen as if inviting him to come in for tea. The entire place whispered *come in and rest.*

He'd rather do just that than go to his grandmother's for dinner. Grammie L. loved a crowd at dinner. A nice private evening with his attractive neighbor was more his speed.

Drinda's place even smelled nice. Peppermint and something sweet. "Were you baking?" he asked.

"Not really. I made some white chocolate peppermint bark to bring. Franny loves peppermint."

He hadn't thought to bring anything. Usually, when he asked, his grandmother said just to bring himself. He should have realized that he could bring something anyway. If they were driving, he'd stop and get flowers.

"What's the frown for?" Drinda asked as she slipped into a navy wool jacket with thin white trim close to the edges and on the collar. It looked like something his grandmother would wear. At least until she buttoned it up and it nipped in at the waist, accentuating her lovely figure.

"I didn't bring anything. I should have."

"This can be from both of us." She handed him a pale blue and pink box tied with a pink and white polka dot ribbon. Coffee Loft colors. She wrapped a red scarf around her neck and tugged on a matching hat and mitts. "I'm all set."

The night was quiet and dark. Large fluffy flakes drifted lazily down from the sky and landed on their shoulders and hats. An air of peace and contentment surrounded them. And he wished he could savor this moment forever. He shoved the thought away. He was turning all girlie.

They walked the first three blocks without saying much. Despite his contentment, the silence began to scratch at his nerves. He was used to the gang at the station who chatted or played games when not on calls. Unless they were sleeping after a tough call the station was always noisy. The quiet between them wasn't uncomfortable, but he still felt like he needed to speak.

"Did you come up with any ideas for dessert?" he asked.

"Really? You're going to drag that up? I want something new, maybe innovative; you want traditional. We're bound to argue. Tonight is supposed to be a nice night with friends." Her frown was like a shot to the chest. Hard and painful.

"I can't help it. I'm a get-things-done kind of guy. Plans need to be made. I thought we could discuss it while we walk."

"Fine."

He knew that fine *never* meant fine, but he kept silent.

"I'm thinking tiramisu. Or a salted caramel torte served with Irish Cream coffee topped with shaved chocolate."

"Again, with the tiramisu. Too fancy." *Why was she so set on fancy?*

"Fancy is good. Elegant is better. This is the perfect chance to showcase my dessert and coffee skills. I need this to be impressive. Ordinary won't cut it." She grabbed his arm and pulled him to a stop.

He turned to look at her.

"Ford, this event is supposed to be romantic and sweet. Men are bringing their ladies here to show how much they care, how much they love them. We can help make this a romantic night to remember." She dropped his arm and started walking.

"We turn left at the corner," he said as he considered her statement. As much as he hated to admit it, she was probably right. He liked variety, why wouldn't other people. This was the twenty-fifth anniversary of the Valentine dinner and dance. Maybe it should be special. Couldn't it be special without being all fancy and froufrou?

"Look at the fairy lights!" Drinda gasped as they rounded the corner onto his grandmother's cul-de-sac. Grammie's house was dead center in the back curve of the small street. As always, it was lit with hundreds of white fairy lights. Drinda clapped her mittened hands together. "They're beautiful. So romantic."

Ford grinned. He'd loved those lights as a kid. Drinda's joy refueled the happiness in simple things he'd lost as he grew older. Grammie L.'s two-story house was flanked by bushes laden with snow-covered white lights. Her deck featured two white-lit trees and her sidewalk was flanked with candle-style outdoor lights on either side from curb to deck. All the lights were white until, in unison, they faded to almost dark and brightened to a pale pink. That was new. Grammie had upgraded her lights. He was miffed that she hadn't asked for help.

"Oh. They're pink now." She stopped and stared at the lights, a breathtaking smile on her face. Her eyes lit with irresistible joy. The lights remained pink for a full minute before taking about fifteen seconds to change back to white. The transitions were slow and subtle.

"I love this so much," Drinda declared. "This is going into my notes."

"Your notes?" he asked.

"I have notes of all the things I want when I finally own my own home. Decorating ideas. Outdoor and indoor features. You know, hot tub outside. Lights on timers. Lots of brightly colored paintings by local artists. That type of stuff."

"You have a list?" The idea of making notes on what he wanted in the future intrigued him. Though if he had a comfy bed and chair, he didn't think he needed much else.

"Yeah, my dream home bucket list. I also have a bucket list of places to go and people to meet. Things to see. Even things I want to try. Like rock climbing."

"Admirable." What else could he say? He was used to getting an idea and setting out to make it happen. As a bachelor, there was nobody to say he couldn't do something. As a landlord and fire fighter, he had plenty of income to do whatever he wanted. Perhaps she didn't have the luxury to just pack up and try something. He was blessed and he knew it, though sometimes it slipped his mind.

Was there anything he'd like to do that should be on a list? Aside from finding someone to spend his life with, he couldn't immediately think of anything. Would being in a committed relationship change how he planned things? Probably. He'd burn that bridge when he crossed it.

"Do you have a bucket list?" she asked, wrapping her arms around herself.

Funny that her question mirrored his thoughts ... as if they were mentally in sync. "I don't. I pretty much do as I want."

She nodded approval. A breeze ruffled her hair, and an enormous shiver shook her entire body.

"You're cold. Come on, my family is waiting. Let's get you inside and out of the cold." He placed his gloved hand on the small of her back and urged her forward. Something about the simple move made him feel protective and masculine. Not that he ever felt emasculated ... this was different and new; like they were connected on a deeper level; on more than the physical plane. He liked it enough that he kept his hand there all the way to his grandmother's front door.

Reluctant to lose the simple contact, he opened the door and gestured for her to enter. A wave of happy noise and the mouthwatering scent of roasting chicken washed over them.

"You don't knock?" She hesitated in the doorway behind him.

"Never. I'm family."

"It's so loud," she whispered.

Chapter Eight

Drinda tried to relax. She really did. Tension was probably rolling off her in visible waves. Six deep breaths didn't help. She just wasn't good at crowds, unless she knew everyone in advance. Ford's family was so outgoing and chatty that her nerves were jumpy. She hadn't expected such a crowd. Eleven people was a lot for a simple dinner. It was more like a full-on dinner party.

Micki was telling a crazy story about a tobogganing near-miss accident with her friends. While she related details, Drinda looked around the enormous living room.

It was decorated in bright florals and a matching deep purple. The walls were a very pale yellow. The tables and knick-knack cabinet were solid wood and obviously well-loved antiques. Adorable little Valentine decorations were scattered about. It was clearly the home of an older, single woman. All that was missing was the old lady smell those homes sometimes had. Her maternal grandmother's house always smelled like lavender and dust. Franny's place was lemony, delightfully infused with roasting chicken, and fresh yeasty rolls.

"Drinda, tell us about yourself," Ford's mother, Kate said.

"Oh." She paused, grasping for something interesting to say. "I own The Coffee Loft. I came to Cherry Lake because my Oma, my dad's mom lives here. I used to spend summers here. Of course, back then she lived on the farm. Now she lives in one of those senior's condos near the main square."

"Those are nice places. Very upscale," Kate said. "We tried to get my mother to move there, but she claims they're for old people, and that she's much too young." She chuckled. "Of course, all her friends live there."

"I wonder if Grammie knows your grandmother," Ford said. "We should ask her."

"What made you open a coffee shop?" Ernest, Ford's father asked, sounding genuinely curious. He leaned forward in his chair, elbows on his knees, and steepled his hands.

"I wanted something different. I've been a baker for years. My friend told me about the franchise and suggested I investigate buying a branch. She thinks my baking skills mesh well with the coffee. It was the perfect way to change careers and escape the city."

"What were you escaping?" Kate asked.

The bold question was startling.

"Mom. Leave Drinda alone. She didn't come to dinner to get the fifth degree," Ford complained. Drinda's heart glowed at his staunch defense of her privacy.

"It's okay. I don't mind." In for a penny and all that. "I was engaged, and my fiancé hated that I worked long hours and strange shifts. He couldn't handle it. I wouldn't give up my job for him. In the end, I realized that it was easier to walk away than to continue to fight. Especially since his schedule was even more erratic than mine. I guess I didn't really love him." She shrugged. "Moving away was ... a fresh start, I guess."

The breakup hurt, but she was over it. She wanted what her parents had. Her mother had kept working as an archeologist and was blissfully happy until she passed. Drinda didn't want to live with the regret of giving up something she loved. Compromise she could live with. Regret was a different story.

"I'm sorry you had a bad breakup," Ford said, squeezing her hand where it rested on the couch between them.

Warmth rushed through her, and she smiled.

If she were looking, Ford would be exactly her type. It was too bad he oversaw her inspections and was her landlord. Of course, he was looking for a stay-at-home wife, according to Annabelle. The very idea was antiquated.

The doorbell chimed, effectively ending the interrogation. She breathed a sigh of relief while Ford's father went to answer the door. He greeted the newcomer and a familiar voice flowed melodically into the room.

"Oma?" Drinda leaped up and raced to the entry. "Oh my gosh! What are you doing here?" She launched herself into her grandmother's arms.

"I came for dinner. Franny and I have been friends for years."

They embraced long and hard. Tears leaked out of Drinda's eyes. "I can't believe that you're here." She leaned back and studied her grandmother. She had a fabulous tan, she looked fit and trim. Her silver hair was cut into a stylish bob. As always, she was bedecked in colorful jewelry and brightly colored clothing. Tonight, she wore a teal sweater dress with navy tights. She was perfect. Warmth flooded over Drinda as her Oma smiled up at her.

"You know me, I love to travel. Paris was amazing, as always. Bora Bora was incredible. It is good to be home and to see you again." She slipped out of her jacket and handed it to Ford's father. "Just look at this tan."

"I love it. You look great. I'm so jealous."

"Maybe next time you'll come with me." Oma grinned.

"Oma, do you know everyone?" she asked.

"I sure do. We all go way back."

101

Franny hurried out of the kitchen. "Great, you made it just in time. How was your trip?" She pulled Olive to the kitchen. "You can help me serve." She grabbed her friend by the arm and chided, "Do you know how hard it was for me to keep our friendship secret while I visited the coffee shop? Don't ever do that to me again."

Drinda watched them walk away and couldn't help but grin, even as she dashed away tears of joy at seeing her Oma for the first time in nearly a year. What were the odds that her new friend Franny was also her Oma's friend? Life was bizarre.

"Are you okay?" Ford asked, striding up and laying a comforting hand on her shoulder.

"Never better. That's my Oma. I loved the summers I spent on her farm when I was a kid." She stared into the doorway to the kitchen, hoping for another glimpse of her beloved relative. She'd missed her dreadfully.

"That's awesome. Come on. Let's get you a tissue, then we can eat."

Ford helped her, Franny, and Oma into their seats and pushed their chairs in before pouring wine. He said grace with an eloquence and gratitude she hadn't expected. She sat between her grandmother and Franny. Being across from Ford was both torture and relief. She was glad she didn't have to sit close and smell his clean soapy scent but watching him smile and laugh was hazardous to her heart and equilibrium.

Dinner was a laughter-filled rowdy event. Drinda slowly lost her self-consciousness around the cheery group and laughed along with everyone else.

She couldn't keep her eyes off Ford. The man was dangerous. She wanted to flee from his vicinity, and she wanted to crawl into his lap and cuddle.

This was not good.

Not good at all.

She put up a mental wall and another around her heart. She wasn't going to let Ford in. There was too much between them, the least of which was her reluctance to enter another relationship with a man who had an erratic schedule. She'd been down that road before and had no intention of going there again.

She'd find a man with a stable nine-to-five position. Someone she could count on to be home when she needed him there. With her crazy early schedule, a man with a regular job was the only way having a family would work, and she fully intended to have at least two children. She loved kids.

"How about you Drinda?"

"I'm sorry. What was the question? I guess I'm a bit overtired. I was up extra early." She faked a yawn and picked up her water.

"Do you have a date for the Valentine's dinner?" Franny asked.

She choked on her water. After half a dozen rough coughs she managed to catch her breath. "Goodness, no. I can't date that day. I'm not opposed to dating in general, but I cannot possibly date on the night I'm serving dessert."

"What are you serving?"

"Something traditional," Ford blurted. She glared at him.

"Something different. Maybe even innovative. I'm testing several new recipes. I intend to bring samples to the next planning meeting. We can let the board decide." She gave Ford a take that look. He opened his mouth to protest but Oma interrupted him.

"What a great idea!" she enthused. "I can't wait. Nothing breaks up a boring meeting like a good dessert." She rubbed her belly in anticipation.

"You're on the committee?" Drinda asked. How had she not known this? They'd had two meetings and not once was her grandmother mentioned. She gave Franny a questioning look.

"Of course. I started the whole event. I'm surprised you didn't know."

What else didn't she know?

After entirely too much food and maybe one too many glasses of wine, she struggled into her coat.

"Here, let me help," Ford offered. He held the shoulders of her jacket and helped her slide her arms inside. He stepped around her and straightened her lapels. She looked up at him.

Their eyes locked for a heartbeat. Then two more. The bright blue of his eyes darkened. Her breath rushed out in a soundless gasp. She leaned toward him. She had to taste to see if he was as delicious as he looked.

His pupils dilated and he bent closer.

"Leaving already?"

They jerked apart.

So close!

Saved by Ford's father. She frowned.

What was she doing? She had no business kissing Ford. None. Not even a little. She was losing her marbles. But boy-oh-boy, had she ever wanted to.

"Unfortunately, I do have to go." She cleared the frog from her throat. "I have to work tomorrow."

"Doesn't the shop open later on Sunday?" Ernest asked.

"It does." She focused on buttoning her jacket to hide the heat in her cheeks. The man had almost caught her kissing his son! They weren't even dating.

Her mind whirled and spun out of control.

Dating Ford. Long winter walks. Dinner and movies. Video game dates. Cuddled up on the couch watching old cop shows. Getting together with friends.

Stop! Don't even think about going there.

And yet, she did. In a matter of seconds, she saw an entire future with Ford.

It made no sense. They bickered over dessert. She wouldn't give up her career. He had an antiquated notion of a stay-at-home wife.

Still, he was great company. They shared a lot of interests. He was good to his mother and grandmother. He had everything she wanted in a man.

He was perfect for her ... and nothing close to what she needed.

Chapter Nine

Drinda stumbled through the snow and up the front step. She jabbed her key at the lock. *Cupcake liners*, she was tired. So tired. Exhaustion beat at every pore of her body. And hunger. She'd feel better once she ate ... if she could muster up the energy to order something. She sure didn't have the strength to cook. Not after her busiest day yet. Elation battled exhaustion. If this kept up, she'd be a success! She'd had to put in an extra supply order and have it rushed in. She'd never survive if her coffee shop ran out of coffee beans.

Maxi was a great help today, but she was still in school and was studying for a big exam. Drinda had sent her home with the admonishment that school came first.

"Hey, Drinda. How are you?"

She jerked around, nearly falling off the step. "Oh. Ford. I didn't hear you come up."

"Sorry about that. Lost in thought?" he asked.

She clutched the railing for stability and looked at him. He wore a navy-blue fire department-issue winter jacket, heavy looking pants, and thick boots. Despite the snow dusting his hair and shoulders, he looked ready to tackle anything.

"Just tired," she said without meaning to.

"Long day?" He stopped where the sidewalk split to go to their separate doors and looked up at her.

"A very good day but busy. So busy." She grinned. "That's a good thing."

"I'm glad business is good. Have you eaten?" he asked. "I was about to order something. Maybe pizza. Maybe sushi. I'm too lazy to cook. It's my last day of six. I'm going into four days off. You could join me."

Two-thirds of her wanted to say no. She was exhausted. But she was starving. If he ordered, she could eat. Food would probably revive her enough to feel human again.

"You know what, that would be great. I'm famished. I could eat a Volkswagen."

"Remind me not to give you silverware," he joked. "What do you feel like? I'll order it while you change."

"Change?"

"Honey, you're covered in flour."

She glanced down and sure enough, her legs were liberally dusted with flour. "Oh my. I had no idea. I wonder when that happened." She rolled her eyes. "It was a day today. I'll eat anything if it isn't too spicy. Order whatever you want."

"Well, options are limited. Indian, Greek, Italian, sushi, pizza."

"Oh, Greek sounds good. Get some souvlaki and maybe some Stifado. I love a Greek stew. Wait, I didn't know we had a Greek restaurant."

"Opened last weekend. It's over by the hardware store on Third Avenue. Go, get changed, and I'll order. Did you want wine?"

She hesitated. She didn't drink very often. "One glass, if it's open. If not, I'm more than happy with tea, or decaf."

"You and your coffee," he chuckled.

"Ha. Ha." She wrinkled her nose and jogged inside. He did make her laugh. Probably more often than he wanted to. For a moment, he even took away her worry about Oscar. She hadn't seen him today. She prayed he was okay. Maybe he went home. With that comforting thought wrapped in her heart, she changed and went next door.

She rapped on the door and let herself into welcoming warmth. She kept her thermostat quite low when she wasn't home and the heat blazing inside Ford's place was wonderful after her chilly walk home.

"I'm here," she called and hung up her jacket.

"In the kitchen. Coffee is almost done. Turns out I didn't have any wine. I'll correct that on my days off."

"Not on my account. I rarely drink."

"Me either, but it is good to have a bottle or two on hand. Food's on the way." He slid a tray with nuts and cheeses on the table. "Persephone's is busy. It's going to be an hour and I'm starving. Dig in." He grabbed a few nuts and devoured them one after another. Typical man.

"How was your shift?" She nibbled a cube of gouda.

"Good. We did a fire safety talk at the elementary school. Kids sure do love fire trucks." He chuckled.

They talked and talked and before she realized it, the doorbell chimed. Dinner had arrived. Ford was incredibly easy to talk to. As a bonus, he didn't bring up her inspection, the dessert, or Oscar.

Dinner was delicious.

"I hate to eat and run, but tomorrow is a workday. I'm training a new girl." She stood and cleared her plate.

"How does that feel? Are you nervous?"

She tilted her head and looked at him. "Not really. I'm excited to be busy enough to *need* help. But I'm concerned that things might slow down. It's hard to know where the balance is. Either I'm run off my feet, or I'm paying someone I don't need. Luckily, this is a mother of teens who is returning to work. She's very flexible and she *loves* coffee."

"Sounds like the perfect employee. And trust yourself. You know what you're doing. Your ads are spot on. You do enough promotion, you have sales, and you've captured the teen crowd."

She chuckled. "That I have, even if their drinks are much less complex than they used to be. They're realizing that all those add-ons cost money. I've hired a programmer to add a reward program to my app."

"If I start using the app to order station coffees, will I get those bonus points?" he teased.

"Oh, I never thought of that." Her mind floundered trying to figure out how many people could potentially take advantage of that. Only firemen and police. Neither group was likely to abuse the system and if they did, she'd figure out a plan. "I'll face that when I come to it." She paused. "If it happens. Anyway, I should go." They walked to the front door, and he helped her into her jacket.

"Can I see you tomorrow night?" Warmth rushed down her spine at his warm, welcoming smile. It had just a hint of uncertainty.

"Oh. I can't. I'm spending the night trying out new flavor combinations. I'm wondering about an orange-almond cappuccino. And maybe cinnamon vanilla."

"And chocolate cherry?" His eyes lit with interest.

"Tell you what. If you want to be my official coffee beverage cupper, swing by the store when I close at eight."

"I'll be the perfect victim for your evil potions." He grinned. "I'm immune to caffeine."

"You're right. This is awesome." She flung her arms around him. "Thank you." She dropped her arms. Heat rose in her face. "Um. Sorry about that. I got a little enthusiastic there." She held back a groan.

"No problem here. You can hug this," he gestured to his body with an up and down motion, "anytime you like. I'm open for hugs."

"Um. Good. I'm glad you aren't upset." She looked around the entry, and then past him. Anywhere but directly at him.

"Hey." He cupped her chin and lifted it up. "I like you, Drinda. A lot. I don't mind your hugs. In fact, I'm looking forward to more."

His eyes held something soft and open.

Her heart tripped.

"Yeah, what's a hug between friends?" His brows pinched together. He seemed, dare she even think it, disappointed.

"Gotta run." She whirled around and opened the door. "Thanks for supper and coffee. See you tomorrow."

The frigid winter air chilled her heated face. She stood on the step, eyes closed, face tipped up into the light drifting snow.

"Are you going inside?" he asked.

"Right!" She forgot he always made sure she made it the twelve steps home safely. He was a gem. A keeper. "Night." She raced up her stairs and inside before she could forget the delicious feel of his body against hers.

It took everything he had for Ford not to arrive too early the next evening. He'd spent the entire day in anticipation of seeing Drinda. She drew him in, unlike anyone he'd ever met. He'd dated. A lot. He was no Romeo or serial dater, but he'd been around the block a time or two. But Drinda struck something in his chest that made her irresistible. She was sweet and kind and funny. He pushed the thoughts back and tried to focus on the task at hand. Tax paperwork.

Tax season was nearly upon him, and if he didn't pay attention, he'd screw this up and get hit with a penalty. Worse yet, his grandmother would face a fine. He put on some upbeat classical music and forced himself to focus. Finally, he slipped into the groove. Enough so that he was shocked when his phone timer went off.

"Holy crap," he mumbled and shut off the alarm. He had just enough time for a quick shower and bite to eat before he saw her again. Excitement burned through him like fire through an abandoned building. He was almost giddy. If any of his buddies had acted this way, he'd tease them relentlessly.

"Who cares? I like her. A lot. And I can't wait to see her." He took the stairs two at a time as he raced for the shower. Shower then food. He whistled through his shower. Grinned through dinner and jogged happily all the way to The Coffee Loft. Drinda was just flipping the sign to *Closed* when he arrived.

She swung the door open for him. As always, she wore her work apron and jeans. Tonight, her top was a scoop necked pink sweater that brought out the blue in her eyes, turning them a deep robin's egg blue.

"Perfect timing. I've got the first drinks ready to go." She waved him inside and locked the door behind him.

Most of the lights were off giving the shop an intimate feeling. Was she romancing him? A pulse of pleasure warmed him right through.

"I've set us up here." She pointed to a table close to her work counter. "Take a seat and I'll be right back."

He slipped out of his jacket and sat. He'd never been here late in the day. The place had an entirely different vibe. It still smelled deliciously of fresh, hot coffee. But it felt different somehow. There were tiny white lights strung around the room, close to the ceiling. They made the room glow. Several of her machines had red or blue lights that lit up the space behind the counter. The back of the mug wall glowed as if lit from behind. The entire feeling was intimate and romantic.

She brought over a small tray with three frothy mugs. "Taste one. Sip it first, then stir and sip." Her hands fluttered over the tray after she set it on the counter. She seemed nervous. "Give me your honest opinion. No filter."

He lifted one mug and sniffed if. "Whoa!"

"Too much?"

"Really heavy on the orange." He wasn't sure he even wanted to taste it. Thankfully, she took the mug away. "That's what I thought. Don't even bother tasting. Try the next."

The first sip was pure foam with the barest hint of flavor. So, faint he didn't recognize it. After a stir he detected almond, chocolate, and orange. This is good."

"Good or great?" She sat across from him, her fingers twisted together. Man, she was adorable when she was nervous.

"I'd say good. I'd drink it."

"Not good enough then," she declared decisively as she pushed the final mug toward him.

A sniff revealed the same aromas, but stronger. The first sip was delicious. "I like this." He stirred it up and tried again. Her eyes were wide with anticipation. He schooled his features to show nothing and took another sip. Flavor burst over his taste buds.

"Oh! This is good! It's deep and rich. Almost decadent without being too much." He took another sip.

She reached up and stopped him from taking a third. "I'm glad. That was my favorite." She pulled a small notepad from her pocket and jotted something down. "Don't drink anymore. I've got two more combinations."

"But it's amazing," he griped playfully.

"If you still want it when you're finished being my victim, I'll make a fresh one. Regular or decaf. Let me grab the next one." She scooped the mug out of his hand, put it on the tray and carried it away.

"I was drinking that," he called.

"Tough tookus."

"Tookus?" he asked.

"Backside." She laughed. "You know, like tough cookies, only different." Her rough laugh felt like velvet on his nerves. He could listen to it all day. She didn't laugh enough.

"Fine. I'll wait. I'll just sit here. Dying of thirst." Drama dripped off his words.

"Wow! For a fire fighter, you are a drama llama, aren't you?" She strolled back with three more mugs. "Guess the flavor from the scent."

He inhaled the warmth over the first mug. "Caramel?"

She clapped her hands gleefully. "Right."

He sipped. Sensing she wanted honesty; he offered his unfiltered opinion. "Oh, this is good." He took three big gulps before she slid it from his hands and demanded he try the others. After tasting both he said, "The first is perfect. The second was almost tasteless, and the third was too salty."

She made a fist and yanked it back toward her body. "Yes! You're good at this. So far, you've agreed with me on everything. It's hard to get just the right amount of everything. Salted caramel syrup alone isn't enough. I had to add a bit of salt to make it perfect." She swatted his hand when he reached for the first cup.

"Hey!" He laughed. She was so much fun to tease. "I'm drinking that."

"I thought you wanted the other one."

121

"Can't I have both?" He whined. Her eye roll made him laugh aloud. When she took the mugs away, he followed her behind the counter.

"Staff only," she quipped.

"Train me how to do this. I've watched but I've never done it."

"Really?"

"Really really. I want to learn all about you and what you do. You fascinate me." He hadn't meant to say it, but he meant it. He rubbed his hands together. "I'll wash up." Without waiting for permission, he washed his hands.

"You'll need an apron." She tossed a pink Coffee Loft apron at him. "Put that on."

He slid it over his head and tied it up. He flounced around behind the counter pretending to do ballet. "Does this make me look fat?"

"You look like a doofus." She chortled. "Come on. This is serious business. If you aren't careful, you'll get a steam burn."

He saluted. "Yes, Ma'am."

"You start with the flavor. I put it in first so it spreads evenly through the coffee. One shot of chocolate, like this." She demonstrated. "Now you add the cherry. Try not to get too much up the sides."

She passed him the mug and the bottle of syrup. He managed to decant it without too much mess, though a bit dribbled down the outside.

"Wipe that off so it doesn't spread to everything," she suggested.

She walked him through the steps of making the espresso. From grinding the beans and pressing it into the cup that was attached to the machine. It was called the brew group. Who knew? While it was brewing into the flavored mug, she poured some milk into a stainless-steel pitcher.

"Hold it under the steamer like this. Not too deep, not too shallow." She demonstrated and handed the pitcher to him. "You do it."

He held it under the steamer and milk sprayed everywhere. He jerked back. "Holy smoking ashes!"

He turned. She was doubled over with laughter. He set the pitcher down and put his hands on his hips and glared. "What's so funny?" He feigned anger.

"You!" She choked out a laugh. "You've got milk everywhere. On your nose, on your shirt. Even in your hair." She tossed him a towel.

"What did I do wrong?" he asked as he wiped himself clean.

"The wand wasn't deep enough. Here, watch me." She stepped forward and he stepped behind her to peer over her shoulder. They weren't touching but the heat of her body warmed his. He closed his eyes and inhaled. She smelled of coffee and strawberry shampoo. Mm.

"Are you watching?" she asked over the noise of the steamer.

He opened his eyes and looked at her. She had lowered the pitcher and was looking up at him over her shoulder. Irresistible. Slowly, he lowered his head towards her mouth. Her head tipped slightly as he moved closer. She nibbled her lip and leaned in. Just as their lips were about to touch, she jerked back and thrust the pitcher at him.

"Try again. Go deeper, but not too deep. Keep it tilted. You want it to roll over and over to get the best foam."

Disappointed, he did as instructed without failure. What was holding her back? They'd been out a few times. Coffee. A movie. Even out to dinner once. They'd spent a couple evenings together. He could have sworn she was into him too. What was holding her back?

She sprinkled sweetened cocoa on top using a heart template. She held it out to him. He cupped his hands around hers and lifted the mug to his mouth. Their eyes locked as he sipped the decadent drink. It was too sweet for his taste, but he kept sipping, unwilling to break the connection.

"A bit sweet. Here, you try," he whispered and tipped the mug toward her. Would she share his mug, or would she refuse him?

She said nothing, but as she let him lift the mug to her mouth, she sipped without breaking their locked gaze. Her eyes darkened and her pupils dilated. Slowly, she backed away.

"It's good. But it was too sweet for me. I ... I think it will be popular though."

He didn't say anything. He couldn't. He was trapped in her gaze.

She closed her eyes, and the trance was broken. Disappointment wrapped around his heart. He wanted nothing more than to kiss her. To claim her.

"I guess that's it," she said, her voice barely above a whisper.

"I guess," he agreed without wanting to.

"I need to clean up."

"I'll help." They emptied the mugs and loaded the dishwasher. He learned how to clean the brewer and the steamer. When she went to dump out the cherry drink, he stopped her. "I'll take that to go, if that's okay?"

"But you said it was too sweet."

He shrugged. There was no way he'd admit he wanted it because her lips had touched it. That was insane.

Chapter Ten

Drinda tromped through the lightly falling snow to the door of The Coffee Loft and unlocked the door. It was still dark outside and would be for hours. Five-fifteen was a peaceful time and she'd learned to enjoy the solitude of early morning.

She stepped into perfect warmth and immediately shed her jacket. A programmable thermostat was a true blessing. Standing on the long gray entry mat, she stomped snow off her boots and brushed it off her hair.

It had been snowing for five days straight. Wasn't it time for spring to start popping up? Heaven knows she'd grown tired of cold damp feet and of mopping salt and slush from her floors.

Everything in the shop was just how she left it. No lights on except the emergency exit signs and one small light behind the counter. There were no tracks on the floor. Nothing was disturbed. Perfect. She flipped on the white mini lights behind the stained-glass windows which flanked the front door. It didn't make sense, but she wanted to let the world know she was inside and the lights were a warm welcome in the dark.

She'd spent every minute of the past four days wondering if she'd made a mistake in not accepting Ford's kiss. He'd been in a few times since then, and it had been all she could do not to fling herself into his arms and against his lips. His pull was magnetic. They hadn't managed to get together since that night.

Light scratching and whines came from outside. Oscar. He'd shown up the day after their near kiss. The crazy dog just wouldn't go away. He spent every day sitting at the front of the shop trying to get in. Nobody had claimed him or answered her ads. The forecast was for minus twenty-five tonight. That wasn't fit for man or beast. She was going to have to do something to protect the pup. The question was what?

Maybe she could bring him inside. But how? She didn't dare violate the health regulations and she couldn't take him home.

She shoved the question aside. She had work to do and her mind would worry out a solution to the Oscar

Dilemma while she did it, if she kept her mind off Ford. The first order of business was to start a pot of coffee and then a batch of strawberry valentine muffins.

The smell of fresh coffee was a balm to her soul. It filled her with peace and energy. This, this one perfect moment when the aroma hit her nose, was why she worked such long hours. She wanted to share her love of coffee and baking with the world.

Scratching restarted at the back door as she pulled down ingredients. Oscar had vanished for a couple days, and she'd hoped he had gone home. But he'd returned the day before yesterday, and she'd taken to throwing him the odd scrap. It was probably why he came back and hung around. Despite the scraps, he was looking thinner.

Her chest ached. What could she do?

Looking around as if there could be anyone inside the closed café, she opened the back door and let him inside. She scooped his wriggling body into her arms, laughing when he licked her chin.

"Hold still, you animal. Let me wipe the snow off your feet." She grabbed a rag and cleaned the ice off his paws. With Oscar in one hand, she set down an enormous cardboard box she hadn't gotten around to recycling and placed him inside. He was adorable with his white snout and black ears. "You stay there," she commanded.

His whine cut straight to her heart. "Just a minute while I get you some food." She threw him a few slices of leftover bacon and spread a thick towel in the box while he ate. Fresh water was next. She sat on the floor beside the box, stroking him as he eagerly lapped up the moisture.

"Good boy." He nuzzled her fingers and lay down. "You nap. I'll cook and figure out what to do with you." If an inspector didn't show up, she'd be fine.

After changing her apron and washing her hands, she sterilized anything she or the pup might have touched and then got back to her muffins. By the time they were ready for the oven, she had finished a mug of coffee, and Oscar was sound asleep in his box.

Almost as soon as they came out of the oven, someone pounded on her front door. Oscar perked up.

"Stay, and by all that's edible, keep quiet or I'll have to put you outside."

She hurried to the front though it was still twenty minutes until she opened. Franny stood outside the front door grinning. Drinda flipped the lock and pushed the door open. Every now and then, Franny liked to pop by before she opened so they could spend some quiet time together.

"Hey, what's up? You're early," she greeted her friend.

"I need coffee," Franny's voice rang with desperation. "For me and your Oma. We're headed into the city to shop for our Egypt vacation. We need suitable clothing. Something cool that keeps us covered. We need road sustenance. Got any day-old cookies?"

"Come in."

Oscar whined. Franny's eyes went wide.

"Did you bring that dog in here?" she whispered.

"Sh. Don't tell anyone. It's just until I figure out what to do with him. He's in a box." She crossed her fingers behind her back in silent prayer that Franny would understand.

"Good for you!" She grinned. "Can I see him?"

"Why not?" She shrugged. She was already busted. Caught red-handed. She led her friend into the kitchen. Oscar leaped excitedly and tipped his box over. Water spilled everywhere. Drinda raced to clean it up while Oscar slobbered all over Franny.

Franny's laugh was beautiful. "He's adorable," she giggled. "Such a cutie. Who's a cute boy?" She sat down next to the box and pulled Oscar into her arms. "I miss having a fur baby."

"Oh, you should get one. Maybe take Oscar home with you?" Drinda offered hope soared in her heart.

"I can't. I'm gone too much. I'll be away for almost half of this year. Egypt first. Then the Mediterranean. Bali. Home for a bit then an Alaskan cruise, and two weeks in Florida. I'm much too busy for a pet." She sounded as disappointed as she was excited.

"Wow. So busy. How will you rest?"

"Girlie, I'll rest when I'm dead. Life is for the living. That's my best advice for a happy life. That and find yourself a good man." She paused. "Like my grandson."

"I happen to know that you have at least four grandsons."

"Any of which would be good for you, but Ford would make you an exceptional husband." She stroked Oscar's back though his eyes were closed.

"No, but thanks for the offer." *Would she never quit with the setup attempts?* "I have to figure out what to do with Oscar."

"I suppose you can't keep him here." She set the puppy back in the box and shifted to her knees before rising. "Oh, these old bones," she grumbled lightly.

"I think you get along well. Come out front and I'll get those drinks for you."

"And a couple cookies, please. Maybe some muffins or biscuits. Do you have a basement in this old place?"

"There is, but it's my stock room. And trust me when I tell you that the inspectors went over it with a fine-toothed comb. I can't hide him down there. Besides, that's no life for a puppy."

Franny's parting words were, "I know you'll figure this out. You've got a good heart, just like my Ford. Thanks for the snacks." She lifted the heavy bag of muffins and cookies in salute.

Drinda tried not to think about her neighbor while she was mixing the muffins, after once again sterilizing her kitchen. Their near kiss was firmly stuck in her mind and her heart. She wanted it, but she wasn't going to take it. They had different goals and he had too much power over her life.

She scrubbed and cleaned because she wasn't going to risk contaminated food. Oscar slept on in his box until she opened at seven.

Ford strolled in just after eight ... before she found a place to hide her new pet. Because there was no denying that like the man standing before her, Oscar had stolen a piece of her heart and was destined to stay. Hopefully, the dog would remain asleep until her friend and nemesis was gone. A search of regulations had proved there was no way to have a pet in an eating establishment. In summer she could keep him on her small outdoor patio. In winter Oscar needed to be elsewhere.

"Good morning, Ford," Drinda smiled at him.

"Good morning to you, neighbor." His face lit with a warm, welcoming smile. It felt like coming home and she couldn't help but smile back. Her heart was going soft. She was seriously falling for this handsome fire fighter with his sparkling eyes and generous nature. Guilt scratched at her conscience. She was lying to him about having a dog in the building.

"Hi," she said lamely, unable to think of anything to say. Her heart thundered in her chest. Partly because he was here and had a way of bringing her body to life with nothing but his presence. Partly because she was terrified, he would find Oscar and report her to the board of health. She turned up the radio just a touch in case Oscar woke up and started whining. She liked Ford, they had a real connection, but she had no doubt that he'd stick to the letter of the law on having a dog in the building.

He slid a long list across the counter. "Here's our order."

"I thought today was your last day off?" She read the list and started making the first drink.

"Gibson came down with food poisoning. I was called in. I'm expecting it to be a slow day anyway. Not that you can predict when a fire will break out."

She chuckled.

"That wasn't a joke." His brows knit together.

"Maybe not, but it was funny." Oscar whined and she fired up the grinder to cover it.

"Did you hear something?" He cocked his head like a dog listening for the smallest noise.

"No." She pretended to listen and hoped Oscar would quiet down.

"I'm sure I heard something. Can you shut that infernal noise off?"

"Not if you want these drinks." She started her large grinder to cover any noise when the espresso grinder stopped. She kept the racket going though she was certain the beans would be ground beyond any possible use. A blur of motion flew past.

NO! Her mind shouted.

"What in the world?" He glared at Drinda. "You let him in here?"

"No!" She sighed. "Yes. He was starving. I couldn't stand to see him shivering in the cold. He's really good. He stays in his box."

"Obviously not." He crossed his arms over his chest. "I can't let this go. You know that, right?" He ignored the dog wiggling in excitement at his feet.

Her heart sank to her toes. She hoped that he might let it slide once, because they were good friends, and she thought they were becoming more. "Yeah, I know. But ... please, Ford. Just give me today and I'll get him out of here. He usually stays in his box. I sterilize everything after he gets out. He won't contaminate anything. I promise." She hated begging. But Oscar's unconditional love was more than worth it.

"Who else knows he's here?"

"Just your grandmother. He's been asleep and nobody else saw him. I swear." She didn't think for one moment that begging would sway him but couldn't stop herself. She locked her knees to keep them from trembling. This man controlled so many aspects of her life. He had the power to shut down her business and evict her from her home.

Ford closed his eyes and muttered under his breath. He glared and said, "Get him out of here. I don't care where you take him, but when I come back tomorrow, he better be gone and for the love of my sanity, don't let anyone else see him."

"I promise I'll get him out of here by the end of the day." She smiled. "Thanks for understanding." She poured a cup of drip coffee before speaking again. "I've finished with all the requirements you stated on my evaluation. You can reinspect any time."

"I'll wait until that mutt is gone."

Chapter Eleven

"Hey, Sage. Brad." Drinda greeted her friends in the waiting room at the vet's office. "I didn't know you had a pet." They were an adorable couple. Brad's dark hair made an amazing contrast to Sage's long blonde locks. They wore jeans and brightly colored sweaters, that clashed yet somehow looked good together.

Sage, a medical receptionist, leaped up from her padded vinyl seat, and hugged Drinda. "Just got a cat. We're waiting to get her shots. I didn't know you had a dog." She knelt and fondled Oscar's ear with a grin.

"Yeah. I found this guy. I'm going to keep him until I find his owner. Dr. Walsh is going to check him for a chip and give him the once over before I take him home." She sat across from her friends after checking in with the vet's aide. A gentle tug on Oscar's leash had him scurrying to her side and away from Sage's pet carrier.

She stared beseechingly at Brad. "Please don't let Ford know. I'm not allowed pets and he's my landlord. This is just temporary until I find Oscar's owner." Brad worked alongside Ford, though they were usually on opposite shifts. Still, she couldn't be too careful.

"Well, if it comes down to a dog freezing outside, or keeping a small secret from a coworker, the pup will win every time. I won't lie, but I won't offer up any information either."

Sage and Drinda smiled at him. "This is why I love you," Sage offered and sat down beside him. They held hands and stared besottedly at each other. Drinda let out an envious sigh. That's what she wanted.

It was Drinda's first time at the vet's office. Bright windows displayed the parking lot. The celery green walls were covered in posters about pet care, and with pictures or adorable animal meme posters. There was an alcove of pet supplies that resembled a pet store. Lemony air freshener kept the scent of animals at bay.

"You should come for dinner," Sage said as Drinda sat down. "We've moved into a new place. We decided to save money before the wedding. We're sending out invites soon."

"Dinner invites or wedding invites?" Drinda laughed.

"Both. But dinner is just you, so you can bring Oscar if you want. And" she paused almost like she was nervous. "I was going to ask ... will you be my bridesmaid?"

"What?" It took a minute to process the request. Drinda leaped up and dashed across the small waiting room. "Yes. Yes. Yes. I'd be honored." They hugged and danced giddily about, while Brad rolled his eyes.

"Women," he muttered.

"Oh, you hush," Sage warned. "You love us, and you know it." She jabbed a finger at him. He grabbed it and kissed the tip.

"Who else have you asked?" Drinda wondered aloud.

"Annabelle will be my maid of honor. It's just you two." Her smile was enormous, and her brown eyes sparkled. "He," she jabbed her finger at Brad, "hasn't chosen his groomsmen yet."

"I will. There's no rush. The wedding isn't until July."

"Men!" Sage and Drinda exclaimed together just as the aide called Sage to the back. Brad picked up their pet carrier and followed her to the back of the clinic.

Oscar had no microchip and no tattoo. But he did get a clean bill of health. Drinda had his vaccinations done and took some pamphlets on raising a puppy. Dr. Walsh warned her that he was likely going to be very large.

"He's only about two-months-old. Barely old enough to be away from his mother," the vet said. "I'm guessing he's part husky, a bit of lab, and probably some Great Dane. He'll be enormous."

"Oh my." Her worry passed in a second. "He's just too adorable to resist. I guess if I can't find an owner, I better find a new home. One that allows pets and has a big yard. What should I feed him?"

After a long lesson on the care and feeding of her new friend, they headed home to scour online used marketplaces for a kennel that would fit Oscar when he grew up. It didn't make sense to get one that would fit now, but not later. The cost of having a pet, even a temporary one, would dig deeply into her meager savings. But Oscar was worth it. For now, she'd sneak him into the house inside a sturdy cardboard box.

"Sh. Don't make a sound," she whispered to the cardboard box as she carried it to her back door. "If Ford hears you, I'm sunk. Got it?"

She slipped inside, grateful that all Ford's lights were off. Either he wasn't at home, or he was already in bed. She couldn't leave Oscar outside all night, nor did she dare leave him in the shop without a proper kennel to contain him. She had fed and watered Oscar and let him do his business outside before bringing him home for the night.

She was a fool. She was risking literally everything for a shaggy, adorable puppy. Tonight, she'd keep him warm and quiet and come up with a plan.

She rushed around double checking that all her curtains were shut before unfolding the box flaps. Oscar hopped out with an excited bark.

"Sh," she chided. "Or we'll end up homeless." He raced around her main floor sniffing everything. His nails scrambled on the tile floors, and he padded soundlessly over the tan living room carpet. He hopped up on her couch and turned circles.

"Get down. No dogs on the furniture." She scooped him off and set him on the floor. He scampered behind her to the linen closet. After digging through the piles, she found a worn towel and set it on the floor. "Here, boy." She patted the towel.

He grabbed the towel in his teeth and shook it with a growl. She laughed at his playful game. Crazy dog. She gave him a bowl of water and started searching for supplies.

An hour later she showed him his new house. She had dumped out her biggest bin of Christmas decorations. After cutting a hole for the door, she glued a fleece blanket to the interior and hung a thick chunk of denim as a flap over the door opening. She secured it in place with a couple of washers and bolts she'd found at the bottom of her toolbox. She threw in another fuzzy blanket and a couple of toys she'd bought on her way home.

Oscar scurried in and lay down to gnaw on the chew stick she'd thrown in. He seemed quite content. Her heart fluttered with love for the silly puppy.

She couldn't have Oscar in the shop, but she could keep him warm out back. Thinking ahead, she had food, more toys, a collar, leash, and tether delivered after Ford left the shop. Pawsitively Perfect was the best pet shop ever.

She'd tie Oscar out back where she could keep tabs on him. It wasn't ideal, but it was a good place to start. If it got frigid, she'd bring him inside and lock him in her tiny office. Again, not ideal, but with the new house, it was a workable option. At least as long as Ford didn't show up.

A skitter of unease slid down her spine. Lying went against everything she believed. But lying to the man she was falling for was ... unthinkable. Yet she was going to do exactly that to protect this innocent pup.

Oscar wriggled out of the makeshift doghouse and chased his tail round and round bumping into furniture and yipping.

She scooped him up and cuddled him close. "Hey, little guy. Don't give us away to our grumpy neighbor. He'll kick both of us out and I'm not certain I want to live in a doghouse." She fondled his enormous feet.

Cute though he was, Oscar was going to grow into a large dog. Maybe the vet was mistaken, and he wouldn't get too large. Hiding a puppy was one thing. Hiding a full-sized lab, or bigger, was impossible.

For two nights, she kept Oscar a secret. She snuck him in and out in his little box. She kept him tied up at work and checked on him every twenty minutes. Sage popped in and took him for a walk when Ford was due for his final inspection.

"Where's the dog?" Ford asked as he filled in the final paperwork.

"Outside. Tied up." There was no sense lying, he'd probably already seen Oscar out there by now.

"Where is he at night? I noticed he wasn't there last night." He fixed her with a penetrating stare that stopped her heart for a second.

"I don't see how that is relevant to this discussion. He does not enter the shop. Ever. Not when it is open. Not when it is closed. Though, if he is around in the summer, regulations permit him to be on the patio." She banked her ire and gave him the warmest smile she could muster. "Did you have any other questions?" she asked sweetly.

His brows met in the middle and the corners of his mouth turned down. "No. That's everything." She could almost see the gears turning in his head. She was in trouble, with a capital T.

"You passed your inspection." He handed her the completed form. "You'll get a wall certificate in the mail. Want to have a late dinner together?" he asked.

"Oh, I wish I could. I already have other plans." Plans to play with her dog and keep him quiet. She'd posted on every community page, put an ad in the paper, and hung flyers everywhere. She'd called the shelter, which thankfully wasn't a kill shelter, and left messages with both veterinary offices in town. She'd covered all the bases, but nobody seemed to be missing their dog. At least not this one.

She was keeping Oscar and had begun her search for a pet-friendly home they could move to. She'd be leaving as soon as her lease was up, or sooner if she could manage it without penalty.

"Maybe another night," she offered hopefully. She could get Sage and Brad to puppysit. She'd had tea with them last night. Oscar and their cat Tiara got along well. Puppies and kittens could be friends if brought together before they were old enough to know they were sworn enemies.

She was barely home that night when someone knocked on her door. Luckily, Oscar was a quiet dog. He didn't bark at strange sounds. In fact, he rarely barked at all. He whimpered and growled but she'd only heard him bark three times.

She corralled him into his kennel in the kitchen and peeked out the front door peephole.

Ford!

Flattened frosting!

Just her luck.

She double-checked that the kennel was out of sight and opened the door. "Ford. What's up?"

"I heard a noise and thought that since you were home, I'd see if you had time for tea."

He heard a noise. She never heard him make noise! He could hear her? Shoot! She was in big trouble.

"That's so weird. I didn't hear anything." She would have to keep the radio on to hide Oscar's small noises.

148

"I'd love tea, but I've got a headache coming on and need to get some sleep. Can I get a raincheck on that?"

"Do you need anything?"

Dang. Did he have to be so accommodating? Guilt pooled in her stomach. "No, but thank you. I'll text if I need anything." She needed to get her life together and find a new home.

She gently closed the door. It took him a full thirty seconds to walk away. While he stood there, his expression was comical. Half concern, half total confusion. She stifled a giggle. She missed him. They'd barely been together since their near kiss. She wasn't avoiding him; they were just busy. Okay, she was avoiding him tonight, but that was different.

She turned the radio on low to cover any noise Oscar might make. She cuddled up with a cup of tea and a book and prayed that she could keep Oscar hidden from Ford. What a mess, she was risking her home and her burgeoning relationship with Ford for a dog.

Chapter Twelve

Four days later, Ford jogged up his front steps. He was surprisingly excited about tonight. Dinner with Drinda and then a planning meeting. Only two weeks left until the Big V Day. He was looking forward to it. Both the meeting and the dinner. Drinda would be working the dessert portion of dinner with a couple of staff she'd hired for the event. He intended to hang out in the community center's kitchen and help where he could.

Tonight, however, he had her all to himself. A quiet dinner out. Then maybe relax and watch a movie together. That new superhero movie was out on pay-per-view and they were going to watch it.

He rapped on her door. Inside there was the sound of shuffling and was that shushing? He shook his head. Probably just reflected sound from the car that had just passed. A full half-minute later she opened the door.

"Ford! I wasn't expecting you yet." Her face was flushed, and her hair tangled. She looked like she'd been wrestling.

"I can see that." He winked. She was adorably messy. She seemed approachable and cuddly. "I was just letting you know I'd be a few minutes late. I was at a small fire and need to clean up. Can we make it half an hour?"

"Oh. Yeah. Sure. Half an hour will be great. I can be ready by then. Tell you what. I'll stop over in thirty minutes. That way you don't have to come to my door." Her eyes bulged and she snapped her mouth shut.

Was she nervous?

About a date with him?

Naw. Couldn't be. They'd been out half a dozen times at least, but not in the last few days.

"Sure," he said slowly. "That works. See you in a bit."

He barely had the words out when she shut her door in his face. *What in the world?* He shrugged off a sense of unease and headed for the shower. He had already showered at work, but occasionally, it took more than one to get the stench of burned plastic out of his nose.

He was exhausted. Fighting fires, even small ones, took a physical and emotional toll. Usually, being with Drinda soothed him but after their brief, weird conversation, he was tenser than before.

Was she hiding something from him? Was she seeing someone else? Were they there now? His mind exploded with unanswerable questions. He'd get those answers. Tonight.

He did a few stretches to unwind, then showered. He was just buttoning up his green and white dress shirt when she knocked. Was she early, or was he running late?

Nope. She was early.

They had dinner at The Italian Place on First Avenue, attended a boring planning meeting where details were rehashed over and over, and walked home. The topic of desserts came up and Drinda put the committee off by promising samples at the next meeting. They'd put it to a vote. He wanted standard and traditional, but somehow, he knew he'd lose. Oh well, it wasn't like he was taking a date to the dinner and dance.

"The snow is nice," Drinda commented, looking up at the lazily drifting flakes.

"It's okay." He was tired of snow. It was only the beginning of February, and the snow was knee deep. He shoveled walks every day. Either his or for people who were unable to do their own. He hired a service for his properties rather than do it himself or depend on tenants, some of whom were too elderly to do it themselves. "I admit, it is pretty, but I could use a break from daily shoveling."

"I hadn't thought of that. I guess I'm lucky I don't have to do my own."

"I noticed you've been driving to work." She'd gone from walking everywhere to taking her car. It was weird because while it was snowy, it wasn't cold.

"Um. Ya. I've been sleeping late and taking the car shaves off time in the morning. It's nice to just go to my attached garage and hop into the car. Boom. I'm at work and ready to make coffee."

"I haven't seen you walking much at all."

"I'm-" she paused. "I'm doing yoga and static exercises right now. I ... I like to switch things up."

Her cheeks were pinker than the cold justified. He was trying to trust her but each half-answer and evasion amped up his unease and distrust.

"Makes sense. I guess." She was up to something. They were dating, but not officially, just a few dinners here and there. And that near kiss. Was she seeing someone else? It seemed unlikely. In a town this small, gossip would out her in minutes. He was growing closer to her all the time. He was darn near in love. He stumbled at the thought. *In love? With Drinda?* The idea didn't scare him as much as it should have.

"Shall we watch the movie at your place?" Neither of them had the morning shift. Drinda's new baker took a couple mornings every week so she could sleep in past five.

"No!" She laughed.

It was the fakest laugh he'd ever heard.

"Let's watch at your place." She stuffed her hands deeper into her pockets and bunched her shoulders up.

He'd rather watch at her place where they could cuddle up on the couch together. His recliners were comfortable, but not at all intimate. He'd rather hold her hand or have her snuggled up to his side for two hours. "I prefer your couches," he hinted.

"I had a long day. I'd really like to put my feet up."

"I can rub them for you," he persisted trying to figure out why she was being so insistent. If she was hiding something from him, the truth would come out. It always did. He banked his disappointment, and something close to but not quite anger. "My place it is."

"I'll just grab a snack and be right over. I won't be more than five. I'd love a cup of tea if you're offering." She zipped inside and shut her door.

He stared at her door mired in confusion.

"How was work today?" She slid into a kitchen chair. It was good to be off her aching feet. The kitchen was neat with only a single plate and fork in the sink. There was a napkin holder and napkins on the table that hadn't been there before. They'd always used squares of paper towel instead of napkins. He was classing the place up.

"It started okay. I helped the guys with some shoveling. The hardware store donated a snowblower. It's been a big help, and we finish faster. We can add more people to our list."

"That's wonderful. I love how the station does so much for others. What went wrong?"

"Just a small fire. I know fires are what I do, but I never enjoy fighting them."

"That's understandable." She squeezed his hand in hers.

Oscar made a low bark, and Drinda took a steadying breath. Her heart was pounding. She was certain Ford was on to her and Oscar despite him being quiet and her keeping the radio on to cover any noise. "Are you going to Sage and Brad's wedding?" she asked hoping to distract him.

"Probably. I don't usually do weddings. Women get all clingy and start thinking of the future."

"Didn't you tell me you wanted a family?" It would be disappointing if he changed his mind. She was starting to envision a future with him.

"Yeah, but I don't want to be rushed into it by some romance crazed woman. I swear weddings are like crack to single women."

The comment should have been offensive, but instead, she saw the absolute truth in it. Before she came to Cherry Lake, she knew a dozen women who had chased down prospective husbands at weddings. She laughed. "We could go together. I'd have a date, and you wouldn't be bothered by the chasers," she offered though the wedding was months away. "Though I am in the wedding party. That shouldn't be a problem though."

"Maybe." He seemed distracted. He brought the teapot to the table. Lemon and ginger swirled through the air.

"Oh, that smells delicious."

Cups smacked onto the table followed by sugar, honey, and cream. Ford thumped into his chair with a frown.

"Where's the dog, Drinda?" His fingers tapped on the table. "I've seen him tied up outside the shop when you are at work. He's not there at night. Where is he?" Anger radiated off him in waves.

Whoa!

Cookie crumbs!

He was onto her. For a brief second, she debated lying. "Next door." She hung her head.

He lurched up and his chair flew backward, banging into the wall.

"Dang it. I told you no pets. It's in your lease. You've broken your lease. Expect your eviction notice tomorrow." He crossed his arms over his chest and glared. "I can't believe you lied to me. I thought we were building something together."

"Ford, I can explain-"

He cut her off. "I don't want to hear it. No pets. That's the rule."

Slowly, she rose to her feet and strode to stand right in front of him, so close she could feel his breath on her face. She banked her anger and disappointment in him. She thought he had a warmer heart. All his other actions said so. Aside from his flip-out when she spilled coffee on him, he was reasonable, friendly, and caring. So much for that.

"Maybe I'm the only one having ... feelings. I like you, Ford. A lot. I thought you cared. I would think that if we were building something, you'd cut me some slack. I'm trying to find his owners. I can't in good conscience let him live outside. He's a baby, Ford. A baby!" Her chest hurt and her hands clenched.

"You didn't even ask first." He stepped back and slashed her with a cutting glare.

"Would you have said yes if I did?"

"Probably not. But you could have asked."

She rolled her eyes and his frown deepened until his eyes and mouth were nothing but hard grooves cut into his face.

"I have a no pet rule. For all my buildings."

"And you couldn't amend that? Not even temporarily?" She blinked back tears. There was no way she'd show him that weakness. Tears weren't a weakness but having him see them was. Screw Ford Lunghamer. She was done with him. She jabbed him in the chest, right over his heart. She hit so hard that her finger buckled.

"You don't have it here, in your heart, to let me keep him until I find his owners, or I find a pet-friendly place? No, you're too stuck in your rut." Okay, she was grasping at straws and flinging unproven accusations.

"Drinda," he said, it sounded like a warning.

"Say goodbye, Ford. I'm out of here, and I'm out of your suite. Consider this me giving my notice." She whirled round and headed for the front door.

"You have to put it in writing," he called.

She spun back around and dashed away a tear. "I could have loved you, Ford. But that's done too. Take your suite and stuff it up your ... firehose."

She crashed out the front door, almost feeling triumphant as it slammed shut behind her. "Of all the ...."

She unlocked her door and went inside. After flipping open the kennel, she flopped onto the couch. Oscar raced around the room for a minute before putting his feet on the couch and licking her face.

"It's okay, boy. We'll be fine. We don't need Ford, or his stupid house. At least now we can play in the yard instead of sneaking walks. And no more pee pads.

You can piddle on his lawn." She fondled his ears and sighed.

"Stupid man. I was falling for you." Oh, who was she kidding. She loved him. From his caring nature, right down to his grump when she spilled on him.

Now she was homeless. If she didn't find a place that took pets, she'd have to surrender Oscar to the shelter. Her heart crumbled a bit more.

Chapter Thirteen

For the first time since she opened, Drinda didn't go to work. She let her staff handle everything. She'd never taken an unscheduled day off. Today marked the second day in a row. She stayed in her suite with Oscar. She lay on the couch staring at the ceiling and moping. When he got antsy, she let him run wild in the yard she shared with Ford. At this point, she was so hurt she considered not even clean up any droppings her pet left out there.

Oh, who was she kidding. She wouldn't wish poop on anyone. Not even Ford the Jerk.

Someone knocked on her door. Oscar perked up his ears but didn't bark or whine. He was such a good dog. Quiet and he never chewed on anything he shouldn't. He was the ideal pet even if her jerk landlord disagreed.

They knocked again.

"Open up this door, Drinda," Franny called. "Or I'll call the police to bust it down. My nephew is a cop. He'll do it!"

The last thing she needed was *his* grandmother sticking her nose into things. She was the one who thrust them together in the first place. She struggled to her feet, blew her nose, and tossed the tissue onto the growing pile on the coffee table.

She flipped the deadbolt and went back to the couch. She sat and buried her face in her hands. Nobody needed to see her red swollen eyes.

"What's wrong?" Sage asked after they let themselves in. "I went to the shop, and they said you texted that you weren't coming in." Several sets of boots tromped in.

"That's two days in a row," Annabelle exclaimed.

"We were worried," Franny said as they trooped into the living room. "Are you ill? Do we need to take you to a doctor?"

"I'm fine." The lie slipped easily off her tongue.

"Clearly that's not true." Sage disappeared into the kitchen and came back with rubber gloves and a garbage bag. She swept the tissues into the bag and carried them away. Water ran and something thumped in the kitchen.

Her grandmother and Franny sat on each side of her and wrapped her in a four-arm hug. "It's okay. We can fix it," Franny murmured. Oscar whined and buried his head in Drinda's lap.

"Spill the beans," Annabelle said.

Sage knelt in front of her. "Do you need money? Are you sick? Did someone die?" She blew the questions out in a fast stream. For all that they were rushed, they seemed sincere. They didn't get to spend much time together, but this group of supportive women had become her best friends.

"No. No. No." She burst into tears for the twentieth time since she confessed to having a dog. The room fell silent. Nobody said anything. Nobody moved. Finally, when the tension felt like it would crush her, Oscar barked.

Everyone laughed.

"Okay now. Tell us all about it," Franny urged. "It's not your health, the store, or money. Nobody died." She snapped her fingers. "It's that no-good grandson of mine, isn't it? Oh, I'll rattle that boy's teeth with the tongue-lashing I'm going to give him. Just wait. Mark my words." She huffed out a breath. "I have half a mind to go to the station right now."

She grabbed Franny's arm. "Don't. It's not his fault," Drinda mumbled. She was tempted to cry again at the looks of sympathy and support on her friends' concerned faces. "I brought this on myself."

"What?" "How?" "No way." They all blurted responses at once. Oma shook her head.

"Wait, I'll make tea. I plugged in the kettle when I cleared your tissues." Sage hurried back to the kitchen. Everyone stared at each other until she returned. "Okay, the tea is steeping. Dish."

"Dish?" Annabelle said. "Who says dish these days?"

"Sh. Let the woman talk," Franny chided like the grandmother she was.

Drinda couldn't help but laugh. She let out a watery giggle. "It is my fault. I'm losing my suite. The other day, the day before yesterday, after the committee meeting, Ford realized that Oscar is living here. At least he guessed. I couldn't lie when he asked. I confessed."

"What's the big deal?" Sage wrinkled up her nose. "He's a clean, quiet pet."

"Ford has an archaic no pets policy." Franny tsked. "As if he couldn't change that if he wanted to. He does own the building." She made another sound of disapproval.

"He's kicking me out. He said I'd get an eviction notice." She swallowed the lump in her throat and choked on her tears. "I'm screwed."

"No. You are not. Come stay with Brad and me. He won't mind. It won't be long until you find a place." Sage patted her hand comfortingly.

"Or stay with me," the others chimed in.

Their words should have been reassuring. Drinda gasped; the room suddenly lacked enough air to breathe. Her chest tightened and spasmed. She'd lucked out when she moved to Cherry Lake to open her Coffee Loft, even if their kind offers somehow made her situation more dire.

"It's not that," she managed between tears.

Nobody responded. The silence was heavy with expectation. This was it. These were her best friends. Franny was practically a mother to her. Sage and Annabelle were like sisters. Even her Oma looked on the verge of anger and nothing set her off.

Her voice trembling, she managed to squeak out, "I think I love Ford."

"Holy moly." Sage clapped her hands.

"I knew it." Annabella did an excited dance in her chair, waving her arms over her head like she'd scored a touchdown.

"I knew he was perfect for you," Franny crowed. "Now, we just have to convince him." Her enormous smile doubled her wrinkles yet made her seem much younger.

"Sorry, guys. I'm done with Ford. We had a good thing. A few good weeks. He's easy to be with. He understands me. He makes me laugh. Honestly, I didn't want to fall for him, I couldn't help myself. I thought he felt the same way. We nearly kissed. Twice."

The others feigned shock and she let out a watery laugh. "But if he's going to make me choose between my home and the safety of Oscar, I'm not interested."

Hurt and anger choked off her words. She curled forward into a ball and rocked back and forth making Oscar whine and paw at her thigh. She scooped him up. "Oh, Oscar. It's okay. I'll be fine."

"When do you have to be out of here?" Sage blurted. "I have an idea!"

"I don't know. He said to expect an eviction notice yesterday. It hasn't come yet." She sniffed. "But I think a month."

"Three months is standard if your lease is month to month. At least in Alberta," Annabelle offered. "That leaves you plenty of time to figure things out."

"In that amount of time, you might even bring Ford around."

Drinda leaped up. "I don't want to *bring him around*," she made air quotes. "I don't ever want to see him again. He has no heart."

"Do you love my grandson? I mean really love him. I'm talking marriage, kids, a lifetime together."

The idea of holding Ford's baby in her arms was poignant and sweet. She'd lost that chance. He had ruined it. "It doesn't matter. He wants a stay-at-home wife. I want my career. They are mutually exclusive."

"With true love, compromise can fix anything. Just look at Brad and me. We fought over a lot of stuff before coming together." Sage shrugged. "No human is perfect. You just have the one who's perfect for you."

"Don't give up yet," Annabelle suggested. "Find a new place to live and take it from there. If you remove the housing issue, there's nothing to come between you. At least nothing that isn't fixable. Although I'm with you on this, why wouldn't he just bend the rules for this adorable pup?" She scratched Oscar's head.

"Even if it doesn't work out," Oma said. "You're a lovely and talented woman. Don't sit around wallowing in hurt. The best revenge is carrying on and showing him that he can't hurt you."

"But he did hurt me." How could they not understand her pain? "He didn't even consider bending." She jumped to her feet. "Well screw you, Ford Butthammer. I don't need you." Her friends cheered and she joined in.

After they left, she slunk back to the sofa and huddled under a blanket. The trouble was, she did need him. He filled a hole in her heart she hadn't even known was empty. The pain she felt at his loss echoed with her heartbeats in that newly opened hole like a big bass kettle drum.

Ford leaned on his shovel and stared down the street. He was only half a block from the duplex he and Drinda shared. It was Sunday. Maybe she was at home with her dog. Even his mind sneered the word.

How in the world had a dog ruined their relationship?

Because he'd been a stubborn jerk and refused to bend. It was a wonder Grammie L. hadn't shown up to give him a piece of her mind. She'd been so pleased when it became clear that he and Drinda were dating.

Something smacked into the back of his head.

"What the ..." he whirled round and squatted defensively.

"Dude. Wake up. We're all shoveling and you're standing there mooning over a woman. Get moving," Brad shouted. "We have ten more yards and I have a very hot

171

girlfriend waiting at home. Our days off rarely coincide and I'm not wasting this opportunity for some hot lovin'."

Around them, everyone groaned. Especially Ford and the station's number one bachelor and deputy chief, Gibson. As if on cue, five men bent and formed snowballs and launched the barrage at Brad's head. A free-for-all ensued. They thrashed around the yard ducking and dodging while pitching snowballs at each other. Mayhem reigned until the whoop of a siren interrupted them.

Allison Birks, head of the Cherry Lake RCMP detachment stood between her car and its open door. "Enough of that, boys; or I'll arrest you for causing a disturbance."

Six snowballs rocketed into the passenger door of her car. She didn't even flinch. She just grinned as they went back to work. She locked up her cruiser and let herself into her house on the other side of the street.

Gibson and Brad wandered over to Ford as the others finished the last few feet of sidewalk. "What's with you, bro?" Gibson frowned and scraped a hand over his five-o'clock shadow. "You're totally distracted. I swear a house would burn down around you and you'd never notice."

"He broke up with Drinda," Brad said. "Over a dog." He filled the last word with derision, though Ford knew the derision was for him, not the animal.

"Wait, you mean to tell me Drinda McKenzie, baker extraordinaire is single?" He fist-pumped the air. "I'm outta here. I need to get myself a date."

"Make a move on her and I'll kick your backside." Ford's entire body tensed as a wave of rage washed over him.

"Not done with her yet?" Gibson mocked.

"We're done."

"You and I are done, or you and Drinda? I'm going to need a clear and definitive answer on that." Ford clenched his fists at Gibson's annoying smirk.

"Get stuffed," Ford snapped. "I'm finished. I'll catch you at the station next shift. Stay away from Drinda." He stormed down the street to his duplex mumbling about worthless friends with every step.

Inside, he leaned back against the door and sucked in a breath. "What the heck is wrong with me? Drinda and I are done. Over." He sighed.

He missed her every minute of every day. He'd spent hours over the past few days, watching her stupid dog romp around in the snow. Drinda managed to stay out of sight unless she was picking up after the dog, after Oscar.

Ford relished every single glimpse. He'd taken to walking past The Coffee Loft as often as possible, hoping for a glimpse of her. He was a danged fool and didn't know how to fix things. At least he hadn't followed through on evicting her. That threat had been way over the top. Guilt was his constant companion from the second he'd uttered the words.

He wasn't prone to fits of temper, but she lied to him. She didn't even ask first. She was right, he probably would have said no. He sighed. He'd have done the same thing in her place. Sneak the dog inside and hope for the best. He'd seen the notices all over town. They were in practically every store window. She had even rented one of those mobile signs. But she'd had the dog for weeks now and it was unlikely that she'd ever find its owner.

He just wished he didn't miss Drinda so much.

She wasn't what he wanted. All his life he'd wanted a wife just like his mother. She stayed home until he was in school. Even then, she was home by the time he got home each day. He wanted that security for his kids.

His mind panned over people he'd gone to school with. Hardly any of them had stay-at-home moms and most of them turned out fine. Several fire fighters he knew had working wives and together they managed to handle kids, work, and keep a household. One couple had six kids and they were fine.

But he wanted what he wanted.

It didn't matter that Drinda was funny. Or that they shared a lot of interests. They came from similar backgrounds, though he couldn't imagine practically being raised by his grandparents as Drinda had.

Until he'd met Drinda, he'd been slogging along, day after day, nothing particularly good or bad happening to him. His world had brightened, and his heart lifted the first time they talked. She was bright and sunny. Funny. Smart. Aside from the career thing, she was exactly what he wanted in a wife.

He thumped the back of his head against the door and cussed. Finally, he worked up the energy to take off his outerwear and trudge to the sofa.

He didn't know what to do, all he knew was that Gibson's threat of asking Drinda out had cut right through him. No way in the world was Ford going to let that Lothario, or anyone get his hands on his girl. He just had to figure out how to win her back, without compromising his stance on no pets and a stay-at-home mom.

His heart plummeted to his toes.

He was sunk.

Chapter Fourteen

The week dragged by like syrup in snow. It was hard to believe it was Tuesday again. One full week had passed since their fight. Drinda sighed as she dug through her cosmetics drawer. She wore makeup maybe twice a year. It wasn't her thing. At work, the heat of the steamer wreaked havoc on foundation and mascara. Tonight, she needed the bolstering effect of a painted-on façade. She slathered on foundation and concealer in a vain attempt to cover the bags under her eyes.

She wasn't sleeping well. She'd lived next door to Ford for months now and not once had she heard him make noise at night. Now she swore he was thumping around next door all night long. Either his night habits had changed, or she was imagining things and losing her ever-loving mind. Whatever the truth was, she looked like death and was not going to the planning meeting without an emotional backup in the form of a good concealer.

She waited until Ford left before kenneling Oscar, climbing into her car, and heading to the meeting. She did not want to risk a chance encounter with him. She made a quick stop at the shop to pick up her dessert selections. Tonight was the night. With less than a week left until the big Valentine's event, she was ready and eager to show off what she could do. If she didn't have to talk to Ford while doing it.

The meeting was already in progress when she arrived. She towed her dolly of boxes into the room and took her place next to the committee head. Thankfully she was not beside Ford, nor could she see him from where she sat. Finally, it was time to present her selections.

"Hi," she greeted everyone. "I have four dessert selections for you. If I could have some help to pass out the plates, I'll explain them." Franny and Sage leaped up to assist. They set out the plain white porcelain plates. Each was carefully laid out with four artfully decorated dessert selections.

"If you look at your plate, you'll see a sample of my tiramisu, a mocha caramel cake with whipped frosting, Black Forest cake, and a salted caramel torte. All these pair well with the Irish Cream Coffee I've planned to accompany dessert. With your approval of course. Go ahead and try everything and let me know if you have questions."

"I thought you and Ford were making the decision," the chairman said.

"I told Drinda it was best left up to her. She's the expert," Ford chimed in.

Drinda's jaw nearly dropped. Ford praising her? Was the world ending? Her knees trembled all the way to the coffee pot. She poured a generous cup and laced it with sugar and cream just to delay seeing the expressions on their faces as they tasted her treats. She sipped her sugary drink, hoping it was decaf because the last thing she needed on top of her sleepless nights was caffeine.

"Stop it," she whispered. "You'll do fine." She'd feel better if she knew she had Ford on her side. They might not have agreed on desserts, but knowing he was there, close by and supportive would have steadied her nerves. Too bad that soufflé had fallen.

The room was totally silent except for forks on plates. Unable to stand the suspense any longer, she turned around. Her eyes met Ford's. He smiled and winked.

Her pulse thundered out of control until a sudden calm washed over her. They might not be friends anymore, but it still felt like he had her back. She smiled gratefully.

Ford's night had brightened when Drinda entered the meeting. His heart soared. She was lovely. She was pale and tired looking despite the makeup she'd tried to mask it with. Though clearly exhausted, she was beautiful.

There was a strange comfort in knowing that he wasn't the only one suffering in their separation. Of course, there was a special torture in knowing he was the cause of her exhaustion. It hurt that she didn't give him any further acknowledgment as she returned to her seat, not even another wobbly smile.

Helpless to stop himself, he leaned forward and watched her every move. She twisted a pen in her hands, her knuckles white. She watched everyone eating, her nerves shining in her eyes. When she glanced his way, he gave a reassuring smile. Her answering smile of relief brought every cell in his body to life. There was his girl.

Yeah, he finally admitted it. She was his girl. No matter the circumstances he'd find a way to win her back.

He dove into her desserts. Surprisingly, he loved them all. The Black Forest cake was his favorite, but when wasn't it?

"I vote for the salted caramel torte," his grandmother declared setting off a noisy debate. The only thing the group agreed on was the Irish Cream Coffee. After about ten minutes, it was getting out of hand. Drinda's shoulders inched higher with every passing second. Ford couldn't endure another moment of watching her stress.

He rapped his knuckles on the table. "May I suggest a vote?"

"Good idea." She smiled at him.

Dang, that smile did weird things to his innards.

After three votes it came down to the torte and the Black Forest cake. They went around the table and when it came to him to cast the final ballot, the desserts were tied. He wanted that cake so bad he could taste it.

But he knew that Drinda really wanted to show off with the torte. Both would be good for her business. He didn't hesitate. Not for a fraction of a second.

"I loved the Black Forest cake."

Her face fell.

"But I think the torte is a better choice for a fancy dinner. My vote goes to the torte." A wave of grumbling mingled with a wave of elation. He was almost oblivious to it all. His entire focus was on the unbridled joy and happiness firing in Drinda's eyes.

He'd miss that cake, but he'd done the right thing.

Since the vote was the last thing on the agenda, he smiled at her one last time, grabbed his coat, and left. He grinned all the way home. The elation on her face tickled him. The only question was if it would break a hole in the wall between them.

Work all week was hectic.

Friday was the worst. It was crazy. Someone set fire to a pile of scrap lumber just outside of town. It wasn't a big deal, but they had to ensure it didn't light the adjacent barn on fire. After they finally ensured everything was out, they went back to the station. They'd barely finished restocking and inspecting the trucks when a house fire broke out across town.

The fire was enormous and with six other houses at immediate risk, engines from three stations were called in to control the blaze. It was one of the busiest shifts he'd ever experienced.

He was exhausted and tonight was the Valentine's dinner. For some crazy reason, he'd agreed to be Grammie L.'s date. The worst part? Drinda would be there. He'd called her. He'd texted her. He wanted to apologize and tell her she could stay, and that Oscar could stay too. He wanted to rebuild what they once had, but she was ignoring him. Maybe tonight he could break through to her.

If he couldn't win her over, at least he could tell her that Oscar could stay. They'd be next door where he could watch over them.

He trudged past his living room, remembering all the times they'd laughed and argued over movies. The kitchen table brought memories of decaf and dessert.

And their fight.

He closed his eyes to erase the painful memory and sucked in a few breaths. And smelled chocolate.

Chocolate? What in the world? He glanced around the kitchen.

How had he missed the enormous pink and blue Coffee Loft box on the counter? Fingers trembling with curiosity and excitement, he peeled away the stubborn tape holding the box closed and flipped the lid.

"Black Forest cake?" He blinked. "How in the world?" He groaned. *Grammie L. that's how.* His grandmother had a key to his house. He wanted to be mad, but he was ecstatic.

He was tempted to call and thank his wonderful meddling grandmother. He'd have to hurry to shower and get there on time. He'd thank Grammie L. when he picked her up.

He sliced a generous portion of cake, and ignoring the inner voice that warned him he'd ruin his dinner, or be late, he sat down at the table to savor every bite. He had no idea why Drinda gave him a cake, but at that moment he didn't care. Not one bit.

The cake was rich, moist, chocolatey goodness with just the right amounts of cherries and whipped cream. He managed to pass up the temptation for a second slice and picked up the box to put it in the fridge.

Beneath the box was a pink envelope with his name written in precise feminine script. That was not his mother, nor his grandmother's handwriting. He fumbled the cake, nearly dropping it. He set the box aside and picked up the envelope.

He flipped it over and over in his hands, set it down, and picked it up again.

He needed to get ready for dinner.

He needed to read this.

He blew out a nervous breath and flipped open the unsealed flap. The paper inside was pink with two black and white gnomes on the lower right corner. Cute. Very much Drinda.

Ford

Thank you for swinging the vote in my favor. I know torte wasn't your first choice. I appreciate you giving me the chance to show off my skills. It means a lot. Consider this cake my thank-you.

There was a wide space before the next paragraph as if she'd paused to take a breath before going on.

Please consider this my notice. Oscar and I will be moving out on March 31st. That's more than the required one month notice as per our lease agreement.

Another space. He could almost hear her breathing. Was she upset? The cake sat heavy in his stomach, and he wondered if it would come back up.

I'm sorry things between us didn't work out. Have a good life.

Drinda.

He crushed the note between his fingers and swore. He'd blown it. She was everything he wanted, and he'd blown it by being stubborn. His chest tightened as he smoothed the wrinkles from the letter and slid it back into the envelope.

He could fix this.

He had to.

Katie O'Connor

Chapter Fifteen

Tonight was supposed to be the glorious launch of her dessert catering expansion. Okay, it still was, only she barely cared. She should be elated. That latte had gone sour. She struggled with the final preparations as the crowd filled the community center.

She was not joining them for dinner, though she did have a reserved seat. She was going to hide out in the kitchen, serve dessert and vanish.

This morning, she'd left Ford a cake and a note. She expected him to call. Her optimism was fading.

"What's up boss? Did you forget something at the shop? I could run and get it for you." Maxi, her overeager teenage employee bounced on her feet. Tonight, her hair was bright pink.

"I have everything. I'm just thinking through service. I love your hair."

"Pink for Valentine's, it seemed like the thing to do." She dropped her bibbed apron over her head and tied it at the waist. "If you didn't forget anything, why the long face? You're like totally in the dumps. Did someone die?" She grasped Drinda's arm, her concern etched on her face. She was incredibly caring towards other people.

"Nobody died. This week's been a dumpster fire and I'm ready for it to be over. Dinner. Dessert. Then bed." She didn't have to stay for cleanup. She had used the community center dishes and the committee had hired cleanup staff.

"Oh, is it man trouble? My auntie gets distracted and grumpy when she's got man trouble." She grinned. "Drinda's got man trouble."

"Sh. Someone will hear you." She couldn't help but laugh at the singsong teasing. "Yeah, but keep it to yourself."

"You and Ford? Brutal. You guys are so good together."

"We were good together, but we have irreconcilable differences." *Ya, Ford was a jerk, and you can't fix that.* "I have to find a new place to live. He was my landlord, and he doesn't like dogs."

"How can he not like dogs? Oscar is the best." Maxi, like many of the local teens, had taken to stopping at the back of the store to visit Oscar now that he had a proper doghouse. It took a while to convince the kids not to feed him scraps.

"Not everyone is an animal lover." Why was she explaining her life to a teenager? She sighed again. Maxi might be a teen, but she was intelligent and empathetic.

"I hope Ford realizes what an idiot he is." She washed her hands and said, "What do you need me to do?"

"You can plate the torte, like this." She demonstrated. "I'll prep the mugs with the Irish cream. You can't do that because you aren't legal drinking age." They worked in silence for ten minutes.

"What are you going to do about Ford? Are you just giving up on him?"

"I don't want to, but I don't see another option."

"Maybe you can hook up after your move. You know when you're not under his roof anymore. Then there isn't anything to keep you apart. Right?"

Drinda set the Baileys bottle down. *Was that possible? Was there hope for them?* She shook her head. *Nope. Ford was a jerk. He didn't even give her a chance.*

"I don't think so. I can't be with a man who would let a dog freeze in the snow. We're over."

"But you like him, right? I think you still love him." Maxi gave her a glare that said wise up, get a grip, and I feel your pain. "Right?"

Loving him wasn't the point. She did love Ford, but she had lied to him. He probably wouldn't have been so annoyed if she had asked before bringing Oscar into her suite. He had every right to be peeved.

She closed her eyes and drew in a breath. Being in love and facing differences was way harder than it should be. Maybe that was the point. Maybe her heart was telling her that she needed to get around those differences because she did love Ford. There was no way to deny it. Had she panicked and backed off too soon? Maybe she should fight for him. Lord knows her own parents had survived more than one divorce-worthy argument. Even Oma and Opa had fought in whispers while she was staying with them.

"You're right! I'm not giving up. I'm going to fight," she declared, slapping her hand on the stainless-steel counter making the mugs dance.

"Can you keep it down?" the lead chef for the caterers asked. "We can't disturb the diners."

She mimed zipping her lips. "Sorry," she whispered. "I just had a life altering epiphany. I'll stay quiet." She realized then that the trio of local classically trained musicians were softly playing romantic dinner music as the servers gracefully carried out plates. Dinner had started.

"What are you so happy about?" Maxi asked. "Are you losing your mind? Grouchy and depressed one minute, upbeat and excited the next. Should I be worried about you?"

Drinda grasped Maxi in a tight hug. "Thank you. I don't know exactly which part of your advice hit home, but I realized that Ford is worth fighting for. I'm going for it. Tonight." She did a little dance.

"Yes!" Maxi whispered excitedly and did a dance with just her shoulders. "What's the plan?"

Drinda pursed her lips. "I have no freaking idea. But I'll figure it out. Somehow." She tapped her lip with her finger. "Never mind. How are those desserts coming?"

"Just waiting for the meals to be served so I have more space. This kitchen is tight. By that I mean it's squishy; definitely not cool." They giggled together, hands over their mouths to keep the noise down.

They worked side by side once the meals were served and the servers on a break. "You know what?" Drinda said. "I'm just going to be bold, like a super dark roast, and talk to Ford. I'm still going to move, but I'm going to tell him I like him. What's the worst that can happen?" Disaster scenarios raced through her mind. He could laugh. He could deny her, or say he never wanted to see her again. So much could go wrong. *Sour milk and over-roasted coffee beans.*

"Good for you. I like Ford. He shovels my Gran's walk, and he rescued her cat when it was stuck in a tree. He's a good guy. You're a good boss. You work well together." Her grin was irrepressible.

When had she started taking dating advice from a teenager? One thing was for sure, Maxi wasn't afraid to share her opinions, and she attacked life with gusto, driving hard for what she wanted. Drinda shrugged. She'd had worse advice from more experienced people.

Ford was supposed to be here tonight, with his grandmother, Franny. If he was, maybe they could talk, and dance. She'd like that. A lot. She peeked out the doorway into the dim hall.

Luckily for her, Ford sat across from Franny at a table near the kitchen. His broad shoulders filled out his black suit jacket like it had been molded to him. His dark tie had light pink hearts on it. She never would have figured him for a seasonal tie guy. The sentimental tie touched something inside her and gave her a warm glow.

The flickering battery powered candles on the table lit his face. He was animated in whatever he was talking about. His smile was large, his eyes wide. *Cake pops!* He looked good enough to eat.

Her chest squeezed. She needed this man in her life. Her heart thudded just watching him. There was no way she could walk away without trying to make things right. She owed him an apology.

He looked up and froze, his wine halfway to his mouth. A slow sexy grin spread across his face. It was too dim to see for certain, but she knew he had tiny laugh lines at the corner of his eyes. He tipped his head in an infinitesimal nod and winked.

She leaped back into the kitchen, her heart pounding.

Okay, maybe there was hope for them.

Unless he was just gaming her by showing he knew she was staring.

Dang it. Why couldn't relationships be straightforward?

As the servers cleared the finished dinners, she began decanting the coffee into mugs while Maxi garnished the last of the plates. When everything was perfect, she gave the nod and the servers started out of the kitchen with the first of the plates.

Ford rubbed the ache in his chest as he looked around the busy hall. He wasn't the only person here with someone he wasn't courting. Two of the guys he went to high school with were here with their mothers. One of the bank tellers was here with her grandfather.

This was one of the things he had missed when he was away training. The sense of family and community in Cherry Lake. There was no shame in being at a fancy romantic dinner with your family. Over in the far corner, two female teachers from the high school sat together laughing. He'd dated them both, so he knew they weren't romantically inclined, though the two florists next to them were.

Dang, he loved this town.

Cherry Lake wasn't the only thing he loved.

He loved Drinda and tonight, he was going to prove it. If she'd even talk to him. He'd caught her staring at him. For a moment, he wondered if she was still interested in him, but when she darted back into the kitchen his heart sunk. Now, as he looked at all the couples in love and clearly enjoying their romantic evening, he wished he were anywhere but here.

Jealousy reared its ugly head and the ache in his chest morphed to a knife-like pain. He must have winced.

"What's wrong?" Grammie asked. "You look like you're in agony. Why are you rubbing your chest?" Her eyes widened. "Are you having a heart attack? Do I need to call an ambulance?"

"No!" he shouted, and several heads turned their way. He forced a reassuring grin. "I just swallowed something wrong. It's stuck." He pounded the center of his chest for emphasis. "I'll be fine."

She squinted at him. "If you're sure?" Her face morphed into a grin. "I think I'll eat my dessert over there and then go home. I have no great desire to slow dance with my grandson. Maybe you can find someone else to dance with." She chuckled. "Don't let fear and common sense hold you back, boy. Grow some nards and go after what you want. Nobody loves a coward." Laughing uproariously, she got up, kissed his cheek, and abandoned him in favor of sitting with three of her friends who shared a table for four.

The salted caramel torte was wonderful. Deep and rich but not too heavy to follow his amazing dinner. The Irish Cream Coffee was the perfect accompaniment to the dessert. Drinda had really outdone herself. When the servers had started clearing plates and prepping for the dance, he hadn't seen Drinda except for that one brief glimpse.

What if she'd gone home already? What would he do? He'd have missed his chance.

Well, smoke and ashes to that! He wiped his mouth and tossed his napkin on the table. Two deep breaths steadied his nerves and he stormed toward the kitchen, praying she was there.

He strode through the swinging door into mayhem. People scurried everywhere with piles of plates, setting them on every available surface. Silverware clattered to the floor; plates rattled. People joked and laughed. He scanned the busy room looking for Drinda. His heart dropped.

She wasn't there. He'd missed her. He was too late.

No way!

He turned around and raced through the hall, dashing around groups of chatting people, dodging tables, dancers, and seniors in walkers. He searched frantically for her in the hall, the foyer, and out into the parking lot.

There! His heart soared.

"Drinda," he shouted. "Wait up. I'd like to talk to you."

She froze in her tracks but didn't turn around. Not good, but at least she stopped. Never in his life had he hated parking lots as much as he did at that moment. Too many cars. He edged between tightly packed vehicles. Okay, he had her attention, now all he had to do was figure out what to say.

He stopped four feet from where she was standing beside the open trunk of her little Chevy.

"Can we talk?" he asked her back. He walked toward her, taking in new details with every step. Her shoulders lifted like she was inhaling deeply. Her fingers straightened at her sides and then fisted. Finally, in slow motion, she turned to face him, a nervous look in her eyes. Her hair glistened in the fluorescent parking lights. Her eyes were wary, her shoulders tense.

"Ford," she said at the exact moment he said, "Drinda."

"You first," they said in unison. The clash of words lightened the mood.

"You go first." She gave a rolling motion with her right, uncovered hand.

"You should have mittens." He shook his head. "That's not why I came out here. Sorry." He took a steadying breath. He stuffed his hands into his trouser pockets to keep from reaching out to her.

He opened his mouth and closed it again. The words weren't coming. His apology stuck in his throat like a chunk of unchewed steak.

"Drinda," he said after way too long a wait. "I don't want things to end like this." *Shoot.* "I don't want things to end at all. Keep the dog. Stay in your suite. Stay, with me." He swallowed the emotions threatening to choke him.

"Um. Thanks?" She frowned like she'd been expecting something else. "I already leased a new place."

"No!" He closed his eyes for a second. "I mean, Drinda, I've been a complete and total jerk."

"No argument here." Her lips twitched with the first hint of a smile and hope soared in his heart. He reached out and took her hands. He pulled them together and warmed them between his. "You're frozen."

She lifted one eyebrow.

"Okay, it's my fault you're cold. I'm keeping you out here." He grinned. "Drinda, I've been a fool. I got upset. I understand why you didn't tell me about the dog."

"Oscar."

"I understand why you didn't tell me about Oscar. I'd have said no, and you'd have been in a worse spot. Forget all that. I was being unreasonable. You can keep him." He winced. He was doing this all wrong.

"Look, forget about the dog, about Oscar," he corrected. "This is about you. And me. Drinda McKenzie, I'm falling for you. Hard. And fast, way too fast." Her eyes went wide, but her expression didn't change. *Talk about your poker face!* Dread weighed on his shoulders, dragging him down like a heavy floor on a burned-out support timber.

"Oh, to heck with this," he declared. "I love you." He dropped her hands and grasped her shoulders. Giving her only a fraction of a second to deny him, he leaned in and pressed his lips to his.

Fireworks exploded and he gasped.

She looked as stunned as he felt. He moved forward again, drawing her into his arms. She fit perfectly against him. Her arms slipped up around his neck and her lips brushed his.

His eyes drifted shut. He wanted to watch her expression, but he needed to feel this. He poured every ounce of love he felt into their kiss. Her return kisses and embrace roared heat and caring through him like a runaway fire.

Lord in heaven, this was where he was meant to be. All the years he dated, he was biding time, looking for this. Looking for Drinda. She tasted of coffee and sunshine, and pure sweet heaven.

Something stilled in his restless soul.

He was home.

"Hey, get a room," somebody yelled. It sounded like Gibson. He'd pay for the interruption.

Blushing, Drinda jumped back and started laughing. "Oh, gosh," she blurted between bouts of giggles.

"Get back here," Ford grumbled. "I like having you in my arms."

She wasn't resisting his kisses, and seemed more than comfortable in his arms but hadn't yet said anything about his declaration of love. Was he alone in feeling this? Couldn't she feel it too?

"Drinda, I'm sorry. And I love you. We can work this out. I'll even be flexible on the stay-at-home mom thing. I don't care. I just want you and our future ten children in my life. I'm fine with a career wife." Weirdly, it was the truth. He realized that his resistance to a career wife was nothing more than a barrier to protect his heart. Drinda had scaled that barrier and blown it out of existence.

"Ten? Not likely. Ford shut up and take me inside for a dance. I'd like to dance with the man I love." She paused. "And I don't mean Oscar."

Laughing together, he led her inside and onto the dance floor. As they whirled around to a classic rock ballad, their grandmothers waved gaily at them.

"Nosy old biddies," Drinda quipped and drew his head down for a kiss. He stopped just before his lips met hers.

"Forget about them," he said. "Dance with me and know that we can work out anything. I can compromise."

"Me too. Except on one thing."

"What's that?" he asked, trying not to frown.

"If you don't kiss me right now, I'm out of here."

Laughing he gave in to her demands.

I hope you loved Ford and Drinda's story.

You can read book 1 of the series, *Sugar Cookie Kisses*, here: https://books2read.com/u/496qMJ

Find the rest of the Coffee Loft series here:

https://books.bookfunnel.com/thecoffeeloftseries

About Katie O'Connor

Best-selling author Katie O'Connor lives in Calgary, Alberta, Canada. She married her high school sweetheart and is living her happily ever after. She is the mother of two grown daughters and is extremely proud of her five grandchildren.

She is the founder of The Write Chicks, a private romance writers' group set up with the sole purpose of supporting each other's writing career. Currently, she is past president of the Calgary Association of the Romance Writers of America. In the past, she's been their secretary and has also served on the organizing committee for When Words Collide, a reader and writer conference in Calgary, Alberta.

Katie's career path has been long and twisted, with most of her life devoted to her family. She's been a waitress, chambermaid, cashier, store manager, as well as a lab and X-ray technician. She's been a small business owner and is an avid quilter and crafter.

She's dabbled in writing since high school because something drives her to create stories. She swears it's impossible for her NOT to write. Unsatisfied with one genre, Katie writes contemporary romance, erotic romance, fantasy/paranormal romance, romantic suspense, and erotica.

She believes in all things magical, including dragons, fairies, UFOs, ghosts, and house pixies. But most of all she believes in love, romance, and hope.

Where to Find Katie

Website: https://katieohwrites.com

Email: katie@katieohwrites.com

Mailchimp Signup: http://eepurl.com/Q2nRr

Facebook: http://www.facebook.com/katieohwrites

Bookbub: https://www.bookbub.com/profile/katie-o-connor

Instagram: https://www.instagram.com/katieohwrites/

Goodreads:

https://www.goodreads.com/author/show/5362469.Katie_O

_Connor

Books by Katie O'Connor

Coyote Creek:
A Lesson in Love 1
A Heart Torn Apart 2
A Secret to Shatter 3
A Melody for Christmas 4
A Surrender so Sweet 5
A Place Called Home 6
A Love to Rebuild 7
Coming Home for Christmas 8
Coyote Creek Box Set 1
Coyote Creek Box Set 2

Cherry Lake Fire Fighters:
Sugar Cookie Kisses
Cappuccino Mugs and Fire Fighter Hugs

A Silver Fox Christmas:
Their Christmas Heart
Their Christmas Love
Their Perfect Christmas
A Silver Fox Christmas Box Set

Hearts Haven:
Running Home
Building Trust
Saving Grace
Heart's Haven Box Set

Three Moon Falls:
Fire Magic

Water Magic

Stand Alone Books:
Carly's Heart
Matchmake Christmas
Cupid's Charm
Gingerbread Dreams
Christmas in Silver Creek
Fake Dating at Half Moon Bay
Sleigh Bells Inn
Hearts in the Spotlight
To a Tea
Bulletproof Heart
Protecting Josie
Rekindled Fire

Strawberry Valentine Muffins

Ingredients

1 Tbsp lemon juice
1 cup milk
½ cup butter, at room temperature
      1½ cups white sugar
4 large eggs
2 tsp lemon extract
½ tsp lemon zest
1½ cups chopped fresh strawberries
3 cups all-purpose flour
1 tsp baking powder
½ tsp baking soda
½ tsp salt
12 slices fresh strawberry
1 Tbsp white sugar

Directions
Preheat an oven to 350°F/175°C.
Line 24 muffin tins with paper liners.

1. Mix lemon juice with as much milk as needed to measure 1 cup; let the soured milk stand for 5 minutes before using. Vinegar also works for this.
2. Cream butter and 1½ cups sugar in a large bowl.
3. Beat in the eggs, one at a time. Add the lemon extract.
4. Stir in the lemon zest and soured milk.
5. Gently fold in the chopped strawberries.
6. Mix the flour, baking powder, baking soda, and salt together in another bowl.

7. Stir the butter mixture into the flour mixture until dry ingredients are just moistened.
8. Spoon batter into prepared muffin cups to about ⅔ full.
9. Place a strawberry slice atop each muffin and sprinkle with white sugar.
10. Bake in the preheated oven until a toothpick inserted into the center of a muffin comes out clean, 25 to 30 minutes. Cool in the pans for 5 minutes. Serve warm.

Chocolate Chip Slice and Bake Cookies

Ingredients
¾ cup (170g) unsalted butter, softened
¾ cup (90g) icing/powdered sugar
1 large egg, room temperature
2 tsp vanilla extract
2 cups (250g) plain/all-purpose flour
¼ tsp salt
½ cup (90g) chocolate chips

Instructions
1. Beat the butter until smooth and creamy. Add the icing sugar and beat until light and fluffy.
2. Add the egg and vanilla. Beat until combined.
3. Mix in the flour and salt.
4. Fold in the chocolate chips.
5. Turn the dough out onto a lightly floured surface and shape into a 2-inch wide log.
6. Tightly wrap the log and chill for at least 4 hours, preferably overnight.
7. Preheat the oven to 350°F/180°C.
8. Slice the log into thick slices and place them onto the prepared baking tray. Bake for 12 to 14 minutes until lightly brown around the edges.
9. Allow to cool for 5 minutes before transferring them to a wire rack to cool.